The Hybrid Child

Mary J. Henson

Contents

Chapter 1

A stream of light fell onto the cages that were laced with neodymium, a rare earth metal. She sat there with her specular wings that covered her frail body. The girl seemed almost like an 18 year old. She tucked into the corner shielding away from the dim light that barely helped in seeing through the dark room. She peeked through her wings looking at me, her eyes were very unusual. I didn't get a proper look at it as she immediately hid behind those razor sharp wings. If I hadn't been staring at her since I had been posted here to guard her I wouldn't have seen her eyes. That was her only movement since the past four hours. "Dante!" A voice called out my name. Footsteps thudded behind me, heavy and firm. I arched my shoulders back and stood upright before turning around.

"Yes commander!" I responded in a firm tone, puffing my chest out. I needed to get this right, I need to get out of this hell hole as fast as I can.

"Has it eaten?" He asked, looking at the girl with disgust in his face. He didn't bother to hide the distaste towards the girl. My hands were twitching on the side of my legs to remark on his attitude but I chose to answer his question. I replied and waited for his indication to go away.

The commander asked for the cage to be opened instead. I obliged to his command and stood straight right beside the door. He stepped inside and knelt in front of the girl. Her wings seemed to be higher as though they were in a defensive stance. "Do you want to do this the painless way or you want to do it the fun way?" The commander asked in the softest tone as if he was talking to a seven year old, well clearly not. She didn't reply but instead tried to move away from his touch. He looked over to the soldier beside him, the soldier handed over a knife, I think it is neodymium from the way the girl flinched. From what I have gathered her kind is vulnerable to them.

The commander traced the knife over her jaw and held her by her hair. She showed no movement as though she was taunting the commander to try his worst. The smile on the commander's face was replaced by an angry look and he stabbed her thigh. Blood seeped out of it. The girl's fists tightened but there was still the same taunting smirk on her face. The commander called in a woman, "come on mutt, you think you are so brave? Now, go and cut her fingers. Show me that I can put you in a better place?"

The girl clutched the knife which was handed over to and crawled towards the woman. The commander's smile grew wider the more she moved towards the woman. She stopped in front of the woman and dropped her wings down and looked into the woman's eyes. The woman was held down by two guards and her cries and pleads for mercy fell deaf to everyone's ears. The girl's lower lip seemed to tremble. She dropped the knife onto the ground. She knelt completely down and looked at the ground as though she didn't want to show any weakness in front of them.

She said, "I-I can't do it, I can't hurt her." Before she could look up, the commander charged at the girl kicking her with his leg, and she fell back with a thud.

"You worthless piece of shit! Did I ask you to kill her? No! I only asked you to cut her fingers!"

He picked up the knife that was on the ground and stabbed the woman multiple times in the stomach. Her screams slowly died down with her life. This was an everyday nightmare, this entire place is cursed. The commander turned to the girl with his jaw clenched. The girl let out a whimper but didn't dare look up at the commander. She whispered into the air, "I'm sorry." As though she were begging for forgiveness from the dead woman.

The commander barged out of the cell and yelled, "Starve her!"

I swapped places with another soldier to have my lunch. I didn't have the appetite to eat after what happened. I needed to bring up my humanity, what they do is completely disgusting. Ever since the crash in the Atlantic Ocean they found a pathway to another world, or a parallel universe whatever they call it. Whatever lurks near or around it, is captured and experimented on. Everything around that area is classified and is completely under the control of the military. Only high officials have information on it.

Sneaking in a slice of bread for the girl isn't going to do me any harm. Only if I am careful enough to not get caught. I stuffed a slice of bread into my pocket and went to the cellar. "Hey bro! How's it going?" I called out to the guy who would be guarding the girl next.

"Aye mate! Pretty much the same. The corpse was stinking so I took a break."

"Want me to cover for you?" I asked hoping he wouldn't say someone else already did or suspect me for pulling up something I shouldn't be doing.

"You're more than welcome to!" He said with a grin raising his mug of beer at me. I gave him a thumbs up and winked before I left.

I went to the cell where the girl was at. She didn't move from her spot. I kneeled in front of her. She flinched as I tried to move close to her. "I'm sorry." She sobbed. She didn't move from the same spot she was when the commander had stabbed the woman. Her hand was touching the ground where she dropped her knife. I can't stay here for long, I wouldn't be able to tell her that the woman would be at peace if she died. It was a better option than to stay in this hell.

"Hey...It's ok, listen to me." I whispered out to her. She looked at me, it was the first time I was looking at her eyes. My breath hitched, they were beautiful. Green swirls and blue tinged in them, It looked like dropping a drop of paint with exquisite color into black water. Her pupil seems to be dissolving into the rest of the eye. She seemed to be tensing under my gaze so I lowered my eyes and took out the bread that I had snuck in. She seemed hesitant; in her position who wouldn't be, anything that has a gentle emotion can be a trap for them. I took a bite of the bread to show her that I didn't poison it.

"See, it's safe to eat." I handed out the bread to her again. She snatched the bread out of my hand and took a bite, she paused for a moment and looked at me for a brief moment before hiding behind her wings again.

"That's all I could get. I'll try getting more next time, I can't stay longer." I told her and hurried out to delete the CCTV footage before the guard comes back.

"No." The girl whispered. She didn't look up at me, she stared at the crumbs in her hands. I could hear footsteps approaching. I reached out to her hands to clean the crumbs, she took them away and hissed at me.

"Someone's coming, don't let them see." I whispered to her, afraid for the consequences if they found out. I quickly left the cell before locking it again.

The guy who I covered his shift for entered. "Hey mate! Thanks for the cover, appreciate it." He thanked me. I nodded over to him and rushed to the security office where I could delete the footage.

"Sam! Do you want to take a break? You seem exhausted, man." I told him while propping myself on a chair beside him.

"Uhhh! All this crap just makes me want to go home." He cried into his hands. I laughed and slapped his back.

"Isn't Sarah pregnant? Why didn't you take a leave?" I questioned taking a sip of his drink.

"I tried, they didn't let me. It's so scary being a parent. Sarah becomes a monster when she's pregnant. Her whole face becomes red and starts screaming..."

"It's the usual. She loves you no matter what." I joked, easing his worries. "It's tougher having a nighteen year old."

"Oh! Please.." He stood up to get coffee, I quickly moved to delete the file, just as I was about to click the button Sam turned around and saw me trying to delete the file of me interacting with the girl. "What the fuck have you been doing?" He dropped his cup and quickly took the seat beside me. "Why- What the hell have you been doing with the girl?" He whisper-screamed looking at the screen and immediately deleted the file that I have been trying to delete.

"I'll fill you in later. I kinda need to rush." I quickly came up with an excuse to leave the room. I could trust him right? He seems to hate this place just as much as I do.

Chapter 2

I came home immediately after the incident with Sam. I threw my bag onto the sofa and threw my shoes off. Elvira was scrolling through her phone and smiling to herself.

"Teenagers." I huffed softly to myself. Amanda had just come from grocery shopping.

"Dan!" She yelled at me with a frown on her face. I stared at her with wide eyes. "Why are you yelling?" I questioned. "You are joking." She rolled her eyes before continuing, "What's the difference between you and our only daughter?"

"For starters, One of us provides an income to the family and the other giggles into their phone." I scoffed. I looked at Amanda to find her with a disappointed look on her face. I look at Vira who was now finally not staring into her phone. I switched on the TV and scrolled through the channels.

"Dante Alvin Cillian." Amanda threatened using my full name.

"Ohh!" Elvira started laughing like a hyena "someone's full name is being used." She rolled all over the sofa clutching her stomach. She looked like a wild hyena. Her hair was all over her face and her clothes were wrinkled. Even though she looked like a mess she seemed so perfect. My little girl. I took her into my arms while she was pulling away from me. I messed her hair even more now, she pouted and looked at me with her big doe brown eyes. The only thing she inherited from her mother.

"Dad." She whined, "you messed up my entire hair now it's mess." She continued pulling her hair to a ponytail.

I laughed, "I was just enhancing your cavewoman hair." She huffed and went to her room.

Amanda still stood at her place hiding her smile behind her stern face that she's barely holding. I stood up and went to her and kissed her lips gently.

"The shoes in and the bag off." She said smiling now. I groaned before putting everything in its place and I sat next to my wife pulling her into my lap. She put her head onto my shoulder, "was it worse today?" She asked. She knew that I didn't have the best day today. She turned facing towards me and put her arms around my neck enveloping me into a warm hug. I returned the hug by pulling her closer and I nodded my head not wanting to answer. She rested her forehead against my head, "you stink."

"Way to ruin the moment, wifey." I smiled back. She frowned looking at my face noticing that my smile didn't reach my eyes. She always knew, I didn't have to pretend in front of her. She knows that I don't have a choice in working for the army. She still soothes the ache that haunts me when I finish my shift.

"Don't pretend in front of me please." She begged squeezing my hand. I didn't want to share the horrors that I have seen in the base so I pecked her lips and went to have a bath.

The cold water run through my body. On every scar that traced my skin. I held my dog tag, stared at it with anger and hurt. My hand tightened around the dog tag and the chain wrapped around it squeezed my skin. I closed my eyes and rested my head against the wall. The tears that i have been holding were free I cried silently into the shower until i could no longer feel the tightened chain around my hand.

I stood once again in front of the cage that the girl was prisoned into. No one else was positioned with me today. I took my chances and went closer to the cage. She sat facing towards the black wall and stared at it. I wanted to know what was running through her mind. Does she want to escape from here? Does she want to kill those who have hurt her? Does she want to save everyone else who are trapped here? Is she missing her family? Of course she would miss them. Home is the only place you would feel safe and comfortable. This place isn't some vacation or so what am I even thinking?

"Hey." I called out to her. She turned but with her wings in a defensive stance. I gulped before continuing," I'm Dante. I thought I would talk to you so that it might provide you some kind of comfort." I looked at her to see if she seemed interested in my opening but she seemed unbothered and disturbed.

"What's your name?" I asked since this was only a one sided conversation and it wasn't going to benefit either of us. I hoped that she would give me any kind of answer but she stared at me with dull eyes that looked almost dead. She didn't seem to be keen in having a conversation with me yet I pitied her so I kept talking. I told her about Alvira and Amanda. Maybe it was a wrong idea it might have caused her more pain, she was away from her family and here I was telling her how I had a wonderful family.

I sighed and got up to leave, just as i was about to leave the room I heard her whisper, "Aine."

I smiled to myself and turned around and gave a small nod to show that I appreciate her opening up to me. It was a progress. Today was a bit better than the rest. The gods had other plans; they seemed to not want a happy day. Four soldiers came barging into the room and dragged the girl out by her hair. She tried to fight against them, she squirmed, fought nick and tooth but failed. I rushed out to see where they were taking the girl but I was stopped.

Just then Sam came up to me, "They are taking her to the white room." He said looking at me. He must have seen the questioned look in my eyes.

"Why?" I whispered, "I thought they wanted her as a weapon, to study her not to torture her?" I questioned.

"It seems that the commander has other plans for her." He said before continuing in a sterner voice, " Dante, stay away from her, please do not get attached to her."

Chapter 3

1o months later

Dante was staring into the endless sky. He felt calmness from the wind. For once he felt as though he was far away from all the horror of the base. Aine was never heard after they dragged her into the white room. He felt guilty, she trusted him and he had provided the protection she had hoped for. He had given her false hope that the world is going to be a better place. He sighed and returned back to the base. He saw Sam approaching to him, "meet me in the CCTV room, ASAP." He whispered as he passed by him.

"What's wrong?" I asked taking a seat beside Sam. He rubbed his hands nervously and ran his fingers over his hair.

"She's not dead Dante, they didn't exactly harm her."

"What? I don't understand. Is Aine alive? How do you even know?" A rush of relief passed over, maybe I could ask her forgiveness. A stream of questions invaded my mind.

"I copied the footage of the white room where she was held until now, don't get caught." He said handing me the hard drive. I nodded and took the hard disk, Sam left without saying anything else. I plugged in the hard disk to the laptop and opened the files.

Aine sat in the corner just like she always used to with distrusting looks on her face, When the commander came in the room she bared her fangs. I tried increasing the volume to hear what they were saying, the video must have not had audio in it. There were two other gaurds who have enteredc along with. The ones who worked along with the underground crime control. They werent supposed to be part od this were they? Just then they brought a cage in, inside the dage there was a feral werewolf. I always assumed that they could shift back to a human form; turns out they can't, they are creatures of the night, only know how to destroy and fuck things. This is bad. Aine is barely an adult, they wont stoop so low would they?

My eyes watered. I couldn't handle these pathetic monsters ruined an innocent soul. The room had only the monster and Aine now, the gates of the cage opened and the monstered steped out sniffing the air. It leaped at Aine tearing the white gown that reached her knees, I could imagine the screams of the fear that she felt. Aine tried to crawl out of the monsters grap, she was too weak against that horrid beast. The monster slammed it's cock into her without remorse. Blood trailed down her thighs as she gave into her nightmare. She dung her nails in her palms and bit her tongue to stop her screams. The monster thrives on pain. The more pain she shows the more aroused would it get. It held onto Aine's throat and fucked her until her body gave up. She collapsed onto the floor, but the monster was still not satisfied. It threw her body onto the cage that was laced neodymium. Her face and stomach burned at the contact. The skin turned yellow, i could see the claw marks marred on her soft, pale skin. Blood dried on her breats and her hair tangled in her own blood while the beast is still pounding into her.

I couldn't hd it anymore, I rushed to the basin and pucked my guys out. My heart ached for Aine, for the horrors she had to endure. I made my mind up, I had to get her out of her, I told her that nothing would happen. The guilt eats me inside out, the thought of Elvira crossed my mind. Aine also was a daughter to someone, what if my baby had gone through that sick, vile "experiments". That was the final straw I didn't twice about the consequences. I was going to get her out of this hellhole.

I destroyed the tape and wwnt to get Sam to help me. Sam was waiting out of the room, "Sam, we have to get her out here." I stated with my mind set and nithing could change that decision.

"Are you nuts?" He hollered, "It is impossible, she's pregnant now, the whole unit is secured they plan on creating more hybrids to create an army. There us no way we can get her out." He crosses his arms and tells me.

"She's a child, Sam. What if it was your daughter? What she was taken away for such experiments? To do what create an army?" I asked hus, questioned his ethics.

His eyes softened, "I'll help you."

We made a plan, have an werewolf out would get the unit to rush to sedate the monster. In that 15 minutes we'll get Aine to my house and somehow get her back to her world, her home.

The plan went smoothly, I reached to Aine's room, she was heavily pregnant. My hearted tugged within me, "Aine?" I called out to her. She stared at me, lifeless eyes that once had some emotion. Her eyes started to water but yet there was no change in her facial expressions. I pulled her into my embrace while she remained still in my arms. I got her out through the back door of the army. Somehow got her out of the camp, but it won't be ling before they realise that it was 'me' who got her out.

"Amanda!" I yelled into the house, "hurry!" Amanda came rushing out, she was shocked to see Aine, a winged created, a frail thing who is vroken inside out in my arms. "Hide her! We gave to be quick on the run." I told her holding her shoulder and supporting Aine in my arms. Amanda didn't understand what's going on, she was panicking at the sudden changes and that our entire life would change from now onwards. Vira came down from hearing the commotion, just then Aine's water broke she's going to go into labour. Aine's screams were very loud, she was bleeding everywhere. Amanda looked at me with eyes full of worry, Vira was hold Aine's hand while Aine kept pushing, Amanda mouthed the words to me shaking her head, "She won't make it."

"No, no, no!" I shouted into the air. I knelt to the ground beside Aine, "look at me, Aine. You are a survivor, You are going to make it. You are a warrior god damn it, please don't give. Don't give up now." My voice started cracking. I sobbed into my hands. Vira was scared she didn't understand what's going on but my little girl was so brave both my girls are going to make it.

I held Aine's hand while she was pushing, she was in so much pain. Just as she was about to give up, a cry tore into the scene, the baby was alive. Aine made it, she did it. I wiped my tears with the back of my hand. "Aine, you did it, the baby's alive." She was silent staring at the baby in Amanda's arms.

Amanda handed the baby to me anfrer cutting the umbilical cord with the scissors that she disinfected with alcohol. The baby had big grey eyes, they weren't like Aine's but they were still pretty. "She's losing a lot of blood, Dan." Amanda said, with hurt in her voice.

"No, do something-" my voice of cut off with the banging at the front door.

Chapter 4

Elvira's POV

I was holding the baby that this girl had just delivered. My thoughts were going haywire. What's going on? Why is this happening? My dad went to look through the peephole to see who was knocking on the door. There was utter silence in the room the baby in my arms was sucking onto his fingers and smiling at me. I hid under the dining table. The door broke down onto my dad, four men entered our house armed and uncle sam, was along with them. The tall man came into the room and knocked Uncle sam down and held a gun to his head.

The other two men held down dad and the other one held the gun at my mom. "Dan, stop this nonsense and hand over the creature and my creation." The tall man taunted my dad. My dad held his head high. "So this is how it is." He didn't hesitate to shoot Uncle Sam. Uncle Sam's body fell down with a thud and blood pooled from his head. Mum shrieked and the sight. I held my cry back by biting into my fist.

"No! Sam" Dad cried while the men behind held him back. "You monster, he was going have a child. A family." Dad cried hard. It hurt me to see him break down, he was always happy even when we barely had food and went hungry for nights, he always made a way for us to smile and never did his smile falter.

"If you don't give me what I want, I will put a bullet into wife's head and the hunt down and make you watch Sam's wife and unborn baby die slowly." The bad man said, "we wouldn't want that now would we? Give me the child and the creature."

Aine's chest bardly rised now, she didn't move. "Kill me if you have to" Dad said. The tall man pulled the slide of the gun back and pointed it to mum. Mum closed her eyes and whispered "I love you." I think it meant for both me and dad. I couldn't watch it anymore.

There was a loud bang and my mum fell onto the floor light as a feather. I didn't want to hide like a coward anymore. "Ma!" I screamed as I came out from the table and cried over her. "Ma! Wake up, please don't leave me" I cried into my mum's shirt while her bloodied hand clutched mine and her eyes were onto me with a smile on her face. Dad grabbed the gun from the man who was holding him and aimed it at the tall man. "Vira! Run away now!" Dad screamed at me. He shot the two men who were about to kill us.

"Grab the creature and the weapon." The man ordered and shot dad. Dad crouched down and held his chest that was bleeding heacily now. "Vira, baby listen to me, run away now. Please darling." He cried softly.

"No daddy, I won't leave with you, don't make me do this." I cried holding the baby to my chest who was also crying now. The tall man now pointed the gun at me.

"Elvira! Run away now!" He screamed, sheilding me. I stood up with my legs wobbling. Tears rolled down my eyes. Just as I was about to turn away I heard two bangs. I knew it, my father was gone now. I closed my eyes and waited for the pain to come. I could hear nothing but the baby cry. I turned to see everything was frozen as though time had stopped. Aine was glowing on the sofa, she turned to me and muttered some words that I couldn't comprehend. The air around us began to buzz, she looked at me once more as though to tell me that she's thankful or sorry I couldn't understand which one it was.

My head started to spin I closed my eyes. When I opened them again, I was no longer home but elsewhere. It didn't feel like earth but looked the same. Trees surround me and the skies were orange with huge birds flying though. I tried to step forward, then was it that I realised a bullet grazed my leg, and it was bleeding. I crouched down hugging the baby in my arms. Dropplets of water fell on me, it was raining. I always loved the rain but now I hated it. I screamed my lungs out and cried. I cried until the darkness took over me.

I opened my eyes I wasn't under the sky anymore, The baby, where was the baby, that cost me everything. I shot up and found the baby beside the fire, I rushed and picked him up, who the fuck puts a newborn baby near fire. I looked around and found my self in a cave.

"You are awake," I heard a voice, and as I turned around, my eyes met those of a man standing at the cave entrance. Bathed in the soft, ethereal glow of the cave's ambient light, he appeared almost surreal, like a figure woven from dreams.

Tall and commanding, he possessed a lean yet muscular frame that moved with a graceful fluidity. His chiseled features were flawlessly sculpted, accentuated by a strong jawline and cheekbones that could have been carved by an artist's hand. Strands of raven-black hair cascaded effortlessly across his forehead, framing eyes that held no emotions.

Dressed in garments that seemed to blend seamlessly with the mystique of the cave, he exuded an air of both regality and enigma. A simple yet intricately designed amulet hung from his neck, the only adornment on his person. His presence was magnetic, drawing me in with an intensity that was both exhilarating and unnerving.

But perhaps the most captivating feature was the pair of magnificent wings that extended from his back, their feathers a kaleidoscope of hues that seemed to shift and change as he moved. These wings, both majestic and battle-worn, spoke of a being that had traversed realms beyond imagination.

As he approached, his lips curved into a half-smile, revealing a hint of playful charm that contrasted with the air of mystery surrounding him. His voice, when he spoke, was a soothing melody, each word resonating like a note in a hauntingly beautiful song.

In his gaze, I felt a connection that transcended mere words – an unspoken understanding that hinted at a story far more intricate than the cave's winding passages. With every step he took, he seemed to unravel the threads of my curiosity, weaving them into a tapestry of intrigue that left me spellbound.

This captivating man, an embodiment of allure and enigma, stood before me like a living paradox, a convergence of beauty and secrets waiting to be unveiled in the heart of the ancient cave. In that moment, it became clear that this man, with his alluring presence and tales etched in both scars and wings, was no ordinary being.

"You don't belong here, do you human?" He states more than questioning. "Nor does that mutt."

Chapter 5

"You don't belong here, do you human?" He states more than questioning. "Nor does that mutt." His voice, rich and melodious, resonated within the depths of the cave, sending shivers down my spine. The hybrid baby nestled in my arms squirmed, its innocent eyes gazing up at the winged man. I took a step back, my heart racing, feeling both the weight of his scrutiny and the intensity of his aura.

His wings, majestic and iridescent, shimmered in the dim light, casting an ethereal glow that danced across the walls of the cave. The air around us seemed charged with an otherworldly energy, a testament to the supernatural realm I had stumbled into.

I steadied my voice, meeting his gaze with a mixture of apprehension and defiance. "We might not belong here, but circumstances led us to this place. I mean no harm, and neither does this child."

He arched his eyebrow, a hint of intrigue flickering in his eyes. "Curious. A human who dares to venture where others fear to tread, and a hybrid offspring, no less. What brings you to the city of the damned?"

I took a deep breath, gathering my thoughts before answering. "My journey was one of necessity. A series of events led me here, I wasn't aware that I would be standing in front of and answering an arrogant and cocky winged man."

The man's lips curled into a half-smile, a hint of amusement dancing in his eyes. "Ah, so you find me arrogant and cocky, do you? I suppose that's a fair assessment, given my nature."

I shifted uncomfortably, feeling a tinge of embarrassment at my boldness. "It's not that I find you... well, never mind. The point is, I didn't anticipate encountering someone like you, and I certainly wasn't prepared for this situation."

He chuckled softly, the sound echoing in the cave. "Life has a way of surprising us, doesn't it? Now, tell me more about these 'series of events' that led you and the little one to my domain."

As I recounted my journey, my mother's death, my father's sacrifice, I didn't want to show any sign of weakness in front of this man, I still couldn't figure out if he was a friend or a foe. I could feel his penetrating gaze on me. It was as if he was reading my mind, delving into the depths of my thoughts and emotions. I saw his eyes and looked at his face that look otherworldly, the irony. I built up a wall where he couldn't see that I'm hurting and made sure it stays that way.

His demeanor shifted slightly, a subtle softening of his expression that hinted at a deeper curiosity. "You possess an intriguing aura, human. Your desires and intentions are not hidden from me."

Heat rose to my cheeks, and I looked away, attempting to regain my composure. "I... I don't know what you mean."

He chuckled again, this time the sound carrying a trace of genuine warmth. "You're drawn to me, even if you won't admit it. Your heart's rhythm betrays you, a melody of longing and uncertainty."

I swallowed hard, my heart pounding in my chest. "That's... not the point. We're here because we have no other option."

His wings rustled as he took a step closer, his gaze unwavering. "Perhaps. Or perhaps fate has a more intricate design."

I met his gaze, my eyes searching his for answers that remained elusive. "What do you want from me? And what are you?"

His lips quirked into a half-smile again, his ego evident in the way he held himself. "Want? My dear human, I am a being of many desires and wants. But rest assured, your safety and that of the child remain my priority, whether my motivations are clear to you or not. For What I am, I am a demon."

Elvira's eyes widened from surprise and her initial distress now increased, "A demon? But you seem... different."

"Appearances can be deceiving, that is my first lesson you learn today." He smirked.

There was an air of mystery that surrounded him, leaving me with more questions than answers. The tension between us was palpable, a delicate dance of attraction and resistance that neither of us seemed willing to fully acknowledge. In that moment, I couldn't deny the pull I felt toward him, nor could I ignore the enigmatic allure that surrounded him. Despite his arrogance, there was a depth to him that I yearned to uncover, a story etched in scars and hidden behind the facade of confidence.

Elvira cautiously accepted the cocky demon's offer, though her mistrust of him remained unwavering. She knew that securing their safety was paramount, and if this enigmatic demon could offer protection, she would use the situation to her advantage. Despite her reservations, there was an undeniable undercurrent of attraction between them, a tension that must be destroyed before she becomes a liabilty in this world.

As Elvira took place near the fire and feeding the baby plant sap, she couldn't help but sense the demon's watchful gaze on her. His presence was a constant reminder of the secrets he held, the mysteries he guarded behind those beguiling eyes.

As they sat by a flickering fire in the heart of the cave, Elvira finally decided to confront the demon. "You know, for someone who claims to prioritize our safety, you're remarkably tight-lipped about your own intentions."

The demon's lips curled into a sly smile, his eyes gleaming with a mix of amusement and something deeper. "Ah, my dear Sphinx, you have a keen sense of observation. But some secrets are best left untouched, like the forbidden fruit hanging just out of reach."

She arched an eyebrow, a mixture of frustration and intrigue swirling within her. "Forbidden fruit? Are you trying to be poetic now?"

He chuckled, the sound echoing in the chamber. "Perhaps. But I assure you, my dear, there's more to me than meets the eye. Just as there's more to you, hidden beneath that facade of skepticism."

Elvira's cheeks flushed slightly, a mixture of embarrassment and irritation washing over her. "You're infuriating."

His laughter intensified, a genuine mirth dancing in his eyes. "Ah, but I do enjoy ruffling your feathers. It's a rare sight to see a human challenge a demon with such fervor."

She sighed, her irritation momentarily giving way to a begrudging smile. "You're impossible."

He leaned in slightly, his gaze locking onto hers. "And yet, here we are, bound by circumstance and desire, dancing on the edge of a precarious alliance."

Elvira raised an eyebrow, a glint of mischief in her eyes. "And stop speaking to me as though you are an old man, you seem to be only 5-6 years older than me."

His lips curled into a sardonic smile. "Ah, my apologies. It's easy to forget the fleeting nature of human years. Time has a different way of unfolding for beings like me."

Before she could respond, he unfurled his wings and with a graceful leap, vanished into the night, leaving Elvira alone in the cave. As the silence settled around her, Elvira's thoughts drifted to her own past, the memories of her parents flooding her mind.

She closed her eyes, remembering the warmth of their embrace and the sound of their laughter. They had been her pillars of strength, her guiding light through the challenges of life. But fate had snatched them away, leaving a void that seemed impossible to fill.

Tears welled up in Elvira's eyes as the weight of her loss pressed upon her chest. She allowed herself to cry, her sobs echoing within the confines of the cave, a raw and unfiltered release of grief. The pain was as fresh as ever, a reminder that no amount of time could truly heal the wounds left by the absence of loved ones.

As the tears subsided, exhaustion washed over Elvira. She curled up on the hard ground, tucking in the baby into her warmth, and succumbed to sleep's embrace. In her dreams, fragments of memories intertwined with visions of the supernatural realm, creating a tapestry of emotions that left her heart heavy and her mind restless.

Unbeknownst to Elvira, the demon returned to the cave, his senses attuned to the trace of sadness that lingered in the air. He watched her sleep, her vulnerability a stark contrast to the defiance she often displayed. He reached out and brushed a strand of hair from her face. "It's fascinating to see you cry, little sphinx. I wish I could too." He whispered into the night.

Chapter 6

The next day, as the sun cast a warm glow over the forest, Elvira ventured near the cave once again. To her surprise, she found the demon sitting by a crackling fire, a freshly hunted deer roasting above the flames. The tantalizing aroma wafted through the air, making her stomach growl.

Raising an eyebrow, she quipped, "Cooking, demon? I must say, you're full of surprises."

The demon looked up, his fiery eyes meeting hers. A mischievous smile tugged at his lips. "Ah, human, the elusive wanderer. You seem to have a habit of stumbling upon my endeavors."

She smirked, taking a step closer. "Luck must be on my side, then. Or perhaps your cooking skills are just legendary."

He chuckled softly, a sound that resonated like a rumble. "You give me too much credit. A demon has to eat, you know."

Watching him work, Elvira felt a strange camaraderie forming, an unlikely connection. "I suppose even demons have their domestic moments."

"Careful now," he replied, feigning offense, "you wouldn't want to shatter my fearsome reputation."

As they bantered, Elvira's curiosity got the best of her. "You know, demon, I've been calling you 'demon' all this time. Seems rather unfair if we're going to be sharing a meal."

He leaned back, regarding her with a thoughtful expression. "True. You may call me... Azurael."

"Azurael, huh?" She tested the name on her lips, finding it oddly fitting and then she extended her hand to the demon. "I'm Elvira. Pleased to finally make your acquaintance." He cautiously extended a clawed hand, and she shook it, surprised by its unexpected warmth.

As they sat down to enjoy their meal, Elvira took a bite of the cooked venison and sighed contentedly. "I must admit, Mr. Demon, you do have some skills in the kitchen."

Azurael inclined his head graciously. "Why, thank you, Miss Moonbeam. It's not every day that a demon's culinary talents are recognized."

Elvira chuckled. "Well, consider yourself the official chef of our little cave."

"Ah, what an honor," The demon replied with mock solemnity and Elvira stuck her tongue out.

Elvira watched with a soft smile as the baby's tiny fingers wrapped around her long, brown hair, tugging on it with an innocent curiosity. The baby's laughter filled the air, a melody of pure joy that warmed her heart. Despite the discomfort, she gently untangled her hair from the baby's grip, her affection unwavering.

Observing this interaction, the demon's brow furrowed in confusion. He approached Elvira, his voice a blend of curiosity and concern, "Why do you allow the child to cause you pain? It doesn't seem logical to endure discomfort willingly."

Elvira looked at the demon, her eyes reflecting a deep understanding. "It's not about the pain," she explained, her voice soft. "It's about the connection, the bond we share. This little one doesn't know any better, and I would do anything to make them smile."

The demon tilted his head, attempting to grasp this concept. "Even if it means enduring discomfort?"

"Yes," Elvira replied, her gaze returning to the baby who was now reaching for her hair once more. "Love is often about sacrifice, about putting someone else's happiness above your own. It's about nurturing and caring, even when it's not always easy."

As the baby continued to play, the demon contemplated Elvira's words. A flicker of understanding crossed his features, perhaps a glimpse into the complex and beautiful nature of human emotions.

Elvira's eyes lit up with a sudden realization, a spark of joy igniting within her. "Alvin," she exclaimed, her voice filled with excitement as she looked down at the baby. "Your name is Alvin!"

The demon, Azurael, observed Elvira's elation with a mixture of intrigue and bewilderment. Azurael's gaze shifted from the baby to Elvira, his eyes narrowing as a revelation seemed to dawn upon him. "This child," he began cautiously, "it carries the blood of both werewolves and fae, and not just any fae, but the royal lineage."

Elvira's expression tightened, and a moment of tension hung in the air. Azurael's curiosity got the better of him, and he gently pressed, "How did you come to possess such a remarkable and potentially perilous child?"

Elvira's eyes held a mixture of sadness and determination. She hesitated for a moment before finally speaking, her voice tinged with a hint of secrecy. "I do not wish to talk about it, Azurael."

The demon's wings rustled slightly, a sign of his growing unease. "You must understand, Elvira, that the royal fae have a history of not accepting hybrids. It could be dangerous for the child if their true nature is discovered."

Elvira's grip on the baby tightened, a protective instinct taking hold. "I know the risks," she replied firmly. "But I can't turn my back on this innocent life. I want to take the baby to the royal fae, to give them a chance."

Azurael's expression darkened. "Elvira, I understand your intentions, but it's unlikely the royal fae will be accepting. They may view the child as a threat or an aberration. It could lead to dire consequences."

Despite Azurael's warning, Elvira's determination remained unshaken. "I have to try, Azurael. I can't ignore the potential for acceptance and a better life. Please, take me to the royal fae."

Azurael sighed, clearly torn by the situation. "Very well, Elvira. I will take you to them, but I implore you to proceed with caution. The fae world is complex, and their decisions are often rooted in tradition and politics. I will not save you from their clutches."

As Elvira and the baby embarked on this risky journey, the future remained uncertain. The clash between two worlds, each with their own prejudices and beliefs, hung in the balance, leaving Azurael and Elvira to navigate the treacherous path ahead.

As Elvira and Azurael ventured deeper into the city of the damned, an eerie atmosphere settled around them. The air grew thick with an otherworldly tension, and the once-dilapidated buildings seemed to pulse with a malevolent energy. Unnatural shadows danced on the walls, and the ground beneath their feet rumbled with an ominous foreboding.

Suddenly, a haunting howl echoed through the desolate streets, sending a shiver down Elvira's spine. Azurael's wings twitched, and his gaze sharpened as he scanned the surroundings. "We're not alone," he murmured, his voice tinged with caution.

From the shadows emerged a formidable creature, its form twisted and distorted by dark magic. It towered over them, with jagged, obsidian-like scales that glinted with an unsettling iridescence. Its eyes burned with an unholy fire, fixed on Elvira and the baby with an unmistakable hunger.

Azurael stepped forward, his wings unfurling as he assumed a protective stance. "Stay close, Elvira," he warned, his voice steady despite the palpable danger that hung in the air.

The creature lunged with surprising speed, its claws slashing through the air. Azurael countered with swift and fluid movements, his wings creating a barrier between Elvira and their assailant. The clash was a whirlwind of motion, each strike resonating with a crackling energy that seemed to distort the very fabric of reality.

Elvira's heart raced as she clutched the baby to her chest, her instincts urging her to find a way to contribute. She spotted an old, rusted sword discarded nearby, a relic from a forgotten time. With a determined grit, she picked it up, her hands trembling as she steadied her grip.

Azurael's strength was undeniable, his movements a masterful dance of combat. But the creature was relentless, fueled by a malevolence that defied reason. Elvira seized the opportunity, using the distraction to rush forward, the sword held tightly in her hands.

With a surge of adrenaline, she swung the sword, the blade connecting with the creature's scales. A searing shriek filled the air as the dark magic protecting the creature faltered. Azurael seized the moment, his wings striking like lightning as he delivered a final, powerful blow.

The creature let out a guttural roar before collapsing to the ground, its form dissolving into a swirling vortex of shadow. The air around them seemed to sigh in relief, the malevolent energy dissipating like a dissipating storm.

As Azurael approached Elvira, his form was splattered with dark crimson, his clothes and wings soaked in the blood of the creature they had just defeated. Despite the gruesome sight, Elvira's gaze remained unwavering, her expression a mix of relief, gratitude, and a deep understanding of the violent nature of their encounter.

Azurael's steps were deliberate, his movements fluid as he walked toward her. His obsidian-black wings, still partially spread, glistened with a macabre sheen in the dim light. His breath was heavy, his chest rising and falling as he savored the lingering adrenaline rush of the battle.

Elvira met his gaze, her eyes reflecting a complex blend of emotions. There was no trace of disgust or horror in her features, only a profound connection that transcended the gruesome scene before them. She understood the necessity of the violence, the harsh reality of their world, and the lengths they had to go to protect what they held dear.

As Azurael reached her, Elvira's fingers instinctively reached out, brushing against his blood-stained wings. Her touch was gentle, a silent acknowledgment of the shared experience they had just endured. Azurael's dark eyes softened, a rare vulnerability flickering within their depths as he returned her gaze.

Azurael's grip tightened slightly as Elvira's fingers brushed against his blood-stained wings. He pulled away, his expression clouded with a mix of conflicted emotions. "Elvira," he began, his voice tinged with a somber note, "you shouldn't trust me so much. I'm not a nice being. You should be scared of what I am."

Elvira's eyes held a playful glint as she met his gaze, her lips curving into a wry smile. "Scared of you, Azurael? Oh, I don't know about that. Nice? Well, that's definitely up for debate."

Azurael's brow furrowed, caught off guard by her response. "You don't understand. I've done things that would make your blood run cold."

Elvira's expression softened, and she took a step closer to him, her gaze unwavering. "Azurael, we've all got our demons, figuratively and literally. But I've seen beyond the surface, beyond the blood and battles. You're more than your past. And as for being nice, well, sometimes not being nice is what gets things done."

A faint, almost imperceptible smile tugged at the corner of Azurael's lips. He looked into her eyes, keeping his stance back and said, "There is no threat now, you can rest for a while we should find a place by sundown." And he flew into the skies.

Chapter 7

Elvira found herself alone in the heart of the dense forest, her surroundings enveloped in a quiet, almost mystical ambiance. Her steps were careful as she cradled the infant Alvin in her arms, his tiny form nestled against her chest. The sunlight filtering through the canopy above cast dappled patterns on the forest floor, creating an ever-shifting mosaic of light and shadow.

As the day wore on and Elvira's strength began to wane, she scanned the area for a suitable place to rest. Her eyes fell upon a majestic tree with gnarled roots that seemed to reach out from the ground like ancient fingers. Its towering trunk was adorned with thick, dark bark, and its branches stretched out in a protective embrace, creating a natural sanctuary beneath.

Gently lowering herself to the ground, Elvira settled against the rough surface of the tree's roots, cradling Alvin in her arms. Looking down at Alvin, she realized that she needed to find nourishment for the baby. The sap of certain trees held valuable nutrients and had been used for generations to sustain life in times of scarcity but it wouldn't help in the baby's growth she had to find milk. Her gaze returned to the tree before her, and she noticed a small, oozing wound on its bark from which fresh sap was seeping.

Cautiously, Elvira collected a tiny amount of the sap on her fingertip and brought it to Alvin's lips. The baby instinctively tasted the sweet substance, his lips puckering in surprise before a look of contentment spread across his face. Elvira continued to feed him the sap, watching as his hunger abated.

Elvira found herself alone and vulnerable, cradling the precious infant, Alvin, in her arms. The dense canopy of leaves above cast dappled shadows on the forest floor, creating an atmosphere both enchanting and eerie. Every rustle of leaves seemed to amplify her solitude, a constant reminder of the challenges she faced.

Fatigue gnawed at her as she trudged forward, desperately seeking a haven for herself and Alvin. Her eyes, heavy with worry, scanned the surroundings until they fell upon a majestic tree with gnarled roots and sturdy branches. A mixture of relief and caution swept over her; this tree offered shelter, yet the unknown dangers of the woods remained a nagging concern.

Cautiously, Elvira settled beneath the outstretched branches, her protectiveness towards Alvin guiding her every move. As she nestled him close, a soft cry escaped his tiny lips, a poignant reminder of his dependence. Elvira's heart ached as she glanced around, her desperation mounting. In a moment of sheer instinct, she reached out and touched a nearby tree, collecting a small amount of its sticky sap. With a mixture of hope and uncertainty, she brought it to Alvin's lips, a makeshift offering born out of her sheer determination to sustain him.

Just as a sense of resignation settled upon Elvira, a presence disrupted the stillness around her. A figure emerged from the shadows, a pale man with fiery ginger hair cascading over his shoulders. His attire, a combination of rugged leathers and weapons, gave him an air of both danger and purpose. Elvira's protective instincts surged, causing her to instinctively edge away, shielding Alvin with her own body.

"I mean no harm," the man's voice broke through the tension-laden air, "I couldn't help but notice your predicament. The little one needs proper nourishment, something more than tree sap to thrive."

Elvira's gaze flickered between Alvin and the stranger, uncertainty etched across her features. His words struck a chord within her, a fragile spark of hope in the midst of her despair. She hesitated, torn between the instinct to shield her baby from potential harm and the undeniable truth that Alvin's well-being hung in the balance.

With a gentle yet persuasive demeanor, the man approached, his reassuring words laced with a sincerity that seemed to resonate deep within Elvira's soul. Slowly, her defenses softened, and she nodded in reluctant agreement. Extending a hand, he offered to help her to her feet, his presence a mixture of mystery and reassurance.

Together, they navigated through the heart of the forest, guided by the man's knowledge and Alvin's urgent needs. Emerging from the confines of the wilderness, a bustling market town unfolded before them, a vibrant tapestry of colors and sounds. The scent of freshly baked bread mingled with the laughter of children, a stark contrast to the solitude Elvira had known for so long.

In the heart of the market, the man guided Elvira to a stall laden with an array of nourishing foods. With a tender smile, he helped her select items that would provide Alvin with the sustenance he required. As the food was gathered, a sense of gratitude welled within Elvira, mingled with a newfound trust for the enigmatic stranger who had crossed her path.

The man's eyes crinkled at the corners as a warm smile graced his lips. "I haven't properly introduced myself," he said with a gentle chuckle, his voice a melodic blend of reassurance. "I'm Eamon."

Elvira regarded Eamon with a mixture of curiosity and gratitude, her earlier apprehension slowly giving way to a sense of connection.

"It's a pleasure to meet you, Eamon," Elvira replied, her voice tinged with a touch of timidity. "I'm Elvira, and this little one here is Alvin."

Eamon's eyes sparkled, he inclined his head towards Alvin. "A strong name for a strong little soul," he remarked, his words carrying an air of respect for the child's resilience.

With a graceful gesture, Eamon extended an invitation. "Elvira, would you do me the honor of joining me for a meal?"

Elvira's gaze shifted between Eamon and Alvin, a mixture of emotions swirling within her. The offer was unexpected yet somehow comforting. She considered the idea, her heart torn between caution and the glimmer of camaraderie she felt in Eamon's presence.

Eamon seemed to understand her inner turmoil, his expression patient and understanding. "I assure you, Elvira, the meal is a simple gesture of goodwill. A chance for us to share a moment of respite amidst the challenges of this forest."

A subtle breeze rustled the leaves overhead, as if nature itself conspired to guide her decision. With a hesitant yet genuine smile, Elvira nodded her acceptance. "Thank you, Eamon. We would be grateful for your company."

As they walked together through the bustling market, Elvira couldn't help but feel a sense of wonder at the vibrant sights and sounds that surrounded them. The aroma of hearty stews and freshly baked bread mingled in the air, drawing her senses into a captivating dance. Alvin, nestled securely against her chest, seemed to sense the change in atmosphere.

Eamon's words lingered in the air, a soothing melody that resonated within Elvira's heart. The warm glint in his eyes and the sincerity in his voice were like a lifeline, pulling her out of the whirlpool of uncertainty that had consumed her. The idea of a shared respite, a momentary escape from the forest's trials, was a concept she hadn't allowed herself to entertain until now.

With a hesitant yet genuine smile, Elvira accepted Eamon's invitation, and they ventured deeper into the bustling market town. The rhythmic hum of activity surrounded them as merchants hawked their wares and laughter bubbled like a gentle stream. Alvin, seemingly captivated by the kaleidoscope of colors and sounds, cooed softly in her arms, his innocence a reminder of the simplicity she so desperately yearned for.

As they strolled together, Eamon's presence remained a steady anchor for Elvira. His words had offered her a momentary reprieve from her worries, a fleeting glimpse of connection that seemed to defy the harsh reality of their circumstances. The sun cast a warm glow upon the town, painting everything with a touch of magic that made Elvira's guard waver, if only for a moment.

But just as they turned a corner, the scene shifted abruptly. Instead of the charming eatery she had anticipated, Elvira found herself facing a bustling plaza filled with an air of anticipation. Stalls adorned with various items lined the square, and a stage dominated the center, flanked by a boisterous crowd. Confusion etched across her features, Elvira's eyes widened at the sight that greeted her: an expansive courtyard filled with an array of creatures, cages, and an unsettling air of transaction.

Her heart plummeted as realization dawned upon her—a creature auction. Her stomach twisted with a mix of dread and disbelief. The courtyard was a grim tableau, a stark reminder that even amidst beauty and camaraderie, the world could be a place of darkness and cruelty.

Her gaze moved past the cages of fantastical creatures, each a prisoner of circumstance, until it fell upon a line of females being presented on a raised platform. Their faces bore the weight of unspeakable horrors, eyes hollow and spirits broken. The realization struck Elvira like a dagger to her heart—these women were being sold as sex slaves, stripped of their agency and dignity.

Her heart sank as Eamon's expression shifted from understanding to something far more sinister. The patient demeanor he had worn earlier now seemed replaced by an unsettling intensity. His words from moments ago echoed hollowly in her mind, twisting their meaning into something she hadn't fathomed.

Anguish welled within Elvira, a torrent of emotions surging forth. Her mind raced, and self-recrimination mingled with a burning sense of betrayal. How could she have been so naïve? How had she let her guard down, blinded by a stranger's words and a fleeting sense of trust? The forest's whispers that had once felt like a guiding embrace now echoed as a bitter reminder of her folly.

"Nature was asking me to trust him." she scolded herself bitterly, her inner voice a harsh critic. She had sought solace and protection in the forest, interpreting its signs as a plea to place faith in Eamon.

Yet, in this haunting courtyard, the truth was laid bare—the forest held no allegiance, and its guidance was as capricious as the wind.

Elvira turned to Eamon, seeking answers within his eyes. Her heart sank as Eamon's expression shifted from understanding to something far more sinister. The patient demeanor he had worn earlier now seemed replaced by an unsettling intensity. His words from moments ago echoed hollowly in her mind, twisting their meaning into something she hadn't fathomed. How could she have been so foolish? She scolded herself mentally, her inner voice chastising her for letting her guard down, for allowing herself to be swayed by a few kind words and a warm smile. Nature wasn't guiding her; it was her own desperate yearning for safety and companionship that had clouded her judgment.

Elvira's grip on Alvin tightened as a fierce determination welled within her. Amidst the tension-soaked atmosphere of the creature auction courtyard, a palpable sense of dread hung heavy in the air. Elvira's accusatory words hung between her and Eamon like an unbreakable barrier. The weight of her realization pressed down upon her, igniting a fiery determination that only grew stronger with every passing heartbeat.

But before she could react further, a trio of shadowy figures emerged from the periphery. Swift as the night itself, they closed in, their movements deliberate and calculated. Elvira's heart leapt in her chest as her fingers instinctively tightened around Alvin, a protective instinct that flared to life.

"No! Leave us alone!" Elvira's voice cracked with desperation, her plea ringing out into the courtyard like a cry for salvation.

One of the men lunged forward with surprising speed, his fingers gripping Alvin's blanket-wrapped form. In an agonizing instant, the precious bundle was wrenched from Elvira's arms, a heart-wrenching cry escaping her lips. Her eyes widened in shock and horror as the baby was carried away, her maternal instincts raging against the brutal separation.

"Alvin!" The name tore from her throat, infused with anguish and fury, as she reached out desperately toward her child.

Eamon's face contorted with a mixture of regret and apprehension, his gaze flickering between Elvira and the unfolding chaos. "Elvira, I—" he began, his words choked by the tumultuous turn of events.

But before he could finish, rough hands closed around Elvira's arms, yanking her backward with an uncaring force. She stumbled, her heart pounding like a drumbeat of terror as the reality of her helplessness sank in.

"No, let go of me!" Elvira struggled against the men's iron grip, her voice a desperate plea as she fought to free herself.

The courtyard seemed to warp around her, spinning into a nightmarish dance of shadows and agony. Her body was dragged across the uneven ground, her cries for mercy falling on deaf ears. Her mind raced, her thoughts a cacophony of fear and defiance, as she clung to the remnants of her resolve.

As Elvira was dragged into the depths of the auction's underbelly, a series of dimly lit chambers unfolded before her. The harsh glow of lantern light cast grotesque shapes upon the walls, revealing a scene of grim preparation. Dresses and finery lay scattered about, a cruel juxtaposition against the backdrop of despair that filled the air.

"No! I won't let you do this!" Elvira's voice wavered between anger and desperation as the men forced her into a chair, their movements callous and unfeeling. Two other men held her down, the other man undress her. "What fine breasts you have." He squeezed her left breast. Elvira's face was full of disgust and inside her she feared on what would become of her. The man knelt down and spread her legs apart, horror crept her face, and tried to shut her legs but the men were far stronger.

"Please, don't do this." She begged them tears rolling down her eyes. The man traced her cunt with his fingers. The two men stood behind laughing at the scene.

"Be a good whore for your master." One of the men holder her spit into her face. Elvira couldn't hold back her tears, The man kneeling down licked her pussy and plunged his finger into her. Disgust crawled every inch of her body. She could do nothing but cry.

"You'll fetch a fine price, my dear," one of the men sneered, a sinister grin etching across his face. They left her dressed in the clothing to auction her.

Elvira's chest heaved with labored breaths as her thoughts raced. She was trapped, ensnared in a nightmare beyond her control. The forest's whispers had betrayed her, and her misplaced trust had led her into this abyss.

A mirror before her reflected a haunting image—a young woman, disheveled and distraught, adorned in finery that felt like a cruel mockery of her identity. Tears welled in Elvira's eyes as she met her own gaze, a silent plea for strength and salvation passing between them.

Chapter 8

The dimly lit chamber seemed to hold its breath as Elvira, now dressed in a lavish gown that clashed horribly with her inner turmoil, was led onto a raised platform. Her heart pounded like a captive bird against its cage, her hands clenched tightly at her sides in a futile attempt to control the terror that threatened to consume her.

Whispers of anticipation and greed danced through the air like malevolent specters, mingling with the despair that clung to the captive women around her. The atmosphere was thick with an oppressive tension, the reality of their impending fate hanging heavy as the auctioneer's voice cut through the silence.

"Ladies and gentlemen, esteemed patrons," the auctioneer's words dripped with a sinister enthusiasm, his tone a chilling reminder of the darkness that pervaded the room. "Behold the finest specimen to grace our stage tonight, a gem among gems, a prize beyond measure. Allow me to present the enchanting Elvira, a rare beauty from the heart of the forest."

Elvira's heart hammered against her ribcage as she stood on display, her eyes cast downward in a futile attempt to shield herself from the scrutinizing gazes that bore into her. Shame and anger coursed through her veins, a bitter mixture that threatened to overwhelm her resolve.

But just as the auctioneer's relentless chant began to wrap around her like a suffocating shroud, the air itself seemed to shift. A rumble, like distant thunder, echoed through the chamber, drawing the attention of all present. Murmurs of confusion and alarm spread like wildfire, overshadowing the auctioneer's insidious spiel.

In a violent burst of energy, the chamber's entrance exploded inward, sending shards of splintered wood and sparks of chaos cascading through the air. Amidst the wreckage stood a figure that seemed to emanate raw power, an aura of anger and destruction that was as mesmerizing as it was terrifying.

Auzrael, an angry demon with eyes ablaze like smoldering coals, barged into the heart of the auction with an air of wrathful purpose. His very presence was a tempest, a force of nature that demanded submission from all who dared stand in his path. His wings unfurled in a display of intimidating grandeur, their dark edges slicing through the tense air like a blade.

As his gaze swept over the scene, his fiery eyes landed upon Elvira, her tear-stained face a stark contrast against the opulent surroundings. Auzrael's heart, a place that had long been imprisoned by his own anger, wavered for a fleeting moment as he bore witness to the suffering etched into her features.

The last fragile threads of his restraint snapped. A primal rage surged forth, an explosion of pent-up fury that obliterated reason and sent him hurtling into a maelstrom of violence. With a furious roar, he lunged forward, his very presence a cataclysmic storm that swept through the auction like a reaper's scythe.

The room descended into chaos, the sounds of screams and crashing furniture punctuating the air as Auzrael's wrath carved a path of merciless vengeance. The men who had orchestrated this depraved spectacle met their doom in the form of a relentless avenger, their bodies falling like broken dolls before the might of his rage.

But amidst the bloodshed and tumult, Auzrael's gaze never wavered from Elvira's tear-filled eyes. His fury, once an unquenchable inferno, now burned with a fierce protectiveness, a sentinel's resolve to shield her from the horrors that had nearly consumed her.

As the dust settled and the echoes of violence subsided, Auzrael stood amidst the wreckage, his heaving breaths a testament to the tempest of emotions that raged within him. Auzrael's entrance onto the stage was nothing short of a haunting spectacle. His form was shrouded in an aura of crimson, the evidence of his fury and retribution vividly displayed in the droplets of blood that clung to his dark attire. Every step he took seemed to echo with a solemn resonance, a reminder of the raw power and controlled violence that lay beneath his surface.

In the midst of the dead and bloodied bodies, Elvira's tear-streaked face emerged like a beacon amidst the darkness. Her eyes widened as she took in the sight of Auzrael, his fiery gaze softened with an emotion she couldn't quite decipher. Fear still lingered in her heart, but there was something else, an inexplicable connection that stirred within her, like a forgotten memory resurfacing.

Auzrael's presence commanded the room, and yet, in that moment, he seemed almost vulnerable as he stood before her. Without a word, he stepped closer to Elvira, his crimson-stained hands, and wings bearing testament to the vengeance he had wrought.

Auzrael lowered himself to one knee before her, his powerful form softened by the weight of his emotions. The brutality of his recent actions seemed to melt away in this intimate gesture, leaving only a vulnerable and complex soul before her.

His bloodied hand, which had wielded destruction moments before, now reached out with a tenderness that belied his fearsome reputation. His fingertips brushed against her cheek, tracing a path that sent shivers through Elvira's entire being. The touch was both electric and soothing, a paradoxical blend that stirred her heart in ways she had never imagined.

Elvira's breath hitched, and she held back a sob that threatened to escape her lips. Her wide eyes met Auzrael's, and in that single gaze, a world of unspoken emotions passed between them—pain, longing, and an overwhelming need for solace.

Auzrael's voice, deep and resonant, broke the stillness. "Elvira," he murmured, his words a gentle caress that enveloped her like a comforting embrace.

Her heart clenched at his voice, settling upon her like a warm blanket in a world that had turned cold. The tears she had fought to contain spilled over, rolling down her cheeks as a choked sob finally escaped her lips.

Auzrael's gaze held hers, unwavering and full of understanding. His thumb brushed away a tear, his touch tender and achingly intimate. "Let it out," he whispered, his voice a soothing balm to her wounded soul.

Elvira's voice trembled as she finally let go of the emotions that had been building within her, her sobs echoing in the chamber like a mournful melody. Auzrael's presence felt like an anchor in the storm, a pillar of strength upon which she could lean.

He remained by her side, his hand never leaving her cheek, his gaze unwavering and full of a compassion that seemed to bridge the gap between their disparate worlds.

As her tears subsided, Elvira found herself drawn into Auzrael's embrace, her head resting against his chest. The rhythmic beat of his heart echoed in her ear, a steady reminder of his presence and the newfound connection that had blossomed between them.

Amidst the fragile embrace, as Elvira's tears subsided and the weight of her emotions began to ease, her thoughts turned back to Alvin, her precious baby who had been torn from her arms. Panic surged anew, a wave of desperate concern that threatened to drown her fragile respite.

"Alvin," she whispered, her voice trembling with a mixture of fear and longing. Her grip on Auzrael tightened, her fingers digging into his clothing as if seeking reassurance.

Auzrael's arms encircled her, his touch a lifeline amidst the storm of her emotions. "Elvira," he spoke, his voice a soothing murmur that gently brushed against her ear, "Alvin is safe. I promise you, he is unharmed."

Her head snapped up, her tearful gaze locking onto his with a mixture of disbelief and hope. "Safe?" she repeated, the word feeling foreign and distant on her tongue.

Auzrael nodded, his fiery eyes tender and sincere. "I found him, amidst the chaos, and ensured his well-being. He's with someone I trust, sheltered from harm."

Elvira's heart seemed to skip a beat as the weight of his words settled upon her. Relief flooded through her like a cleansing tide, washing away the fear that had held her captive. Auzrael's presence, once a source of uncertainty, had become her sanctuary—a protector who had extended his shelter to her most precious treasure.

With a gentle yet decisive movement, Auzrael lifted Elvira into his arms, his powerful wings unfurling like the embrace of a guardian angel. The sensation of being carried through the air was both exhilarating and surreal, her heart racing as they soared above the tainted remnants of the auction chamber.

As the world below shrank to a distant blur, Elvira clung to Auzrael, her fingers entwined in the fabric of his clothing. The wind whispered against her skin, carrying with it a sense of freedom and boundless possibility. She gazed down at the forest canopy below, a tapestry of green that seemed to hold both secrets and solace.

Auzrael's voice, a steady anchor amidst the rush of wind, reached her ears. "We're almost there," he assured her, his words a comforting melody that resonated deep within her soul.

Minutes later, Auzrael descended with a graceful glide, gently setting down upon a small clearing nestled within the heart of the woods. The scene before them was a sanctuary—a tranquil oasis far removed from the horrors they had escaped.

Elvira's feet touched the soft earth, and she looked around in wonder. Moonlight filtered through the trees, casting a soft, ethereal glow that illuminated the surroundings. Auzrael's presence beside her was a reminder of the extraordinary bond they shared—a connection that had blossomed amidst chaos and pain.

"I thought you might find solace here," Auzrael explained, his gaze resting upon her with a mixture of concern and quiet understanding.

Elvira's heart swelled with gratitude, a profound appreciation for the demon who had become her unlikely savior. She turned to him, her eyes shimmering with unshed tears, and whispered, "Thank you, Auzrael. For Alvin, for saving me... for everything."

Elvira's whispered words hung in the air like a fragile melody, a testament to the depth of her emotions and the gratitude she held for Auzrael. As her eyes shimmered with unshed tears, Auzrael's typically composed demeanor faltered, his body stiffening almost imperceptibly.

He had faced countless battles, navigated the treacherous terrain of realms both mortal and ethereal, and yet, in this moment, he found himself at a loss for words. The weight of Elvira's appreciation and vulnerability seemed to ripple through him, a powerful current that stirred the depths of his own complex emotions.

For a brief moment, Auzrael's fiery gaze met hers, and within that silent exchange, a myriad of conflicting feelings danced—an echo of his past, a glimpse of his struggle, and a glimmer of a future that had been cast into uncertainty. He was a being forged in the crucible of violence and pain, a demon who had embraced his wrath as both a shield and a weapon. And yet, Elvira's simple gratitude had penetrated the armor he had meticulously built around his heart.

Clearing his throat, Auzrael finally spoke, his voice tinged with a mixture of vulnerability and a touch of self-deprecating humor. "I... I am not accustomed to such... expressions," he admitted, his words carefully chosen, as if he were navigating uncharted territory.

Elvira's gaze held his with unwavering warmth, her eyes a reflection of the genuine connection they shared. "You don't have to be," she replied softly, her voice a gentle reassurance. "Just know that your actions have meant everything to me, Auzrael."

Auzrael's breath caught in his throat, his gaze momentarily dropping to the ground as he grappled with the maelstrom of emotions that churned within him. He had faced demons and gods, wrestled with the darkness that coursed through his veins, and yet, this simple exchange felt like the most formidable challenge he had ever encountered.

With a faint yet undeniable resolve, Auzrael lifted his gaze once more, meeting Elvira's eyes head-on. "Then, I am honored," he said, his voice steadier now, his words carrying a weight that extended beyond their spoken syllables.

A demon approaches them holding Alvin, Elvira takes alvin into her embraced and kisses him all over

As Auzrael and Elvira stood in the moonlit clearing, their shared moment of vulnerability and understanding was interrupted by the arrival of another figure—a demon whose presence seemed to pulse with an aura of intrigue and mystery. Clutched securely in the demon's arms was Alvin, Elvira's precious baby, his innocent eyes wide with a mix of curiosity and wonder.

Elvira's heart leapt at the sight of her child, a surge of emotions rushing through her like a tidal wave. With a gasp, she stepped forward, her arms outstretched as if drawn by an invisible force. The world around her seemed to blur as her fingertips brushed against Alvin's soft skin, a touch that ignited a fierce protective instinct within her.

"Alvin," she breathed, her voice a mixture of awe and tenderness. The baby's name was both a prayer and a promise, a reminder of the unwavering bond that had survived the trials they had endured.

As the demon carefully transferred Alvin into Elvira's waiting arms, a flood of emotions threatened to overwhelm her. Tears welled in her eyes once again, but this time, they were tears of joy and relief. She held Alvin close, her fingers tangling in his soft hair as if imprinting the sensation onto her very soul.

Alvin's innocent gaze met hers, and a heartwarming smile tugged at the corners of his tiny lips. In that precious exchange, a world of unspoken connection passed between mother and child—a shared journey of separation and reunion, of pain and the promise of a brighter future.

Unable to contain her overwhelming love, Elvira leaned down and pressed a series of soft, tender kisses against Alvin's forehead, his cheeks, and the bridge of his button nose. Each kiss was a silent vow, a pledge to protect and cherish the life she held in her arms.

Auzrael, who had been observing the reunion with a mixture of reverence and a touch of uncertainty, took a step back to allow the intimate moment to unfold. The moonlight cast a gentle glow upon the scene, turning it into a tableau of maternal love and unbreakable familial bonds.

As the kisses continued, a warm smile tugged at the corners of Auzrael's lips. In this innocent display of affection, he saw a reflection of the resilience of the human spirit—a testament to the capacity for love and hope even in the face of the darkest of challenges.

As Elvira's tender kisses filled the moonlit clearing, a new presence made itself known—a demon named Behomath, whose arrival sent a ripple of tension through the tranquil scene. His formidable aura was laced with a sense of urgency and concern, a stark contrast to the intimate moment that had been unfolding.

Auzrael, who had been caught up in the emotion of the reunion, turned his attention towards Behomath. His fiery gaze met the newcomer's, a mixture of surprise and curiosity flickering within his eyes.

"Behomath," Auzrael, he addresses the demon who had brought Alvin, his voice a measured rumble that held a touch of wariness. He shifted slightly, his focus momentarily torn between the delicate scene before him and the enigmatic demon.

Behomath's expression remained impassive, his eyes locked onto Auzrael's with an intensity that bordered on urgency. His voice, when he spoke, was a low, rumbling undercurrent that seemed to reverberate through the very air.

"Auzrael, you forget yourself," Behomath admonished, his tone laced with a hint of caution. "You are not just a mere warrior. You hold a title—the Prince and next in line to the throne of Hell."

Auzrael's brow furrowed, a hint of consternation darkening his features. The weight of those words settled upon him, a reminder of a responsibility he had long sought to distance himself from.

"And what does that matter now?" Auzrael's response was tinged with a touch of defiance, his attention still divided between Behomath's words and Elvira's quiet moment of affection with Alvin.

"It matters greatly," Behomath insisted, his voice taking on an edge of urgency. "Your compassion, your softening... it is a dangerous path, Auzrael. You must remember who you are, and the role you are destined to play."

Elvira, cradling Alvin in her arms and unaware of the implications of their conversation, looked between Auzrael and Behomath with a mixture of curiosity and unease. The air seemed to thicken with unspoken tension, and a sense of foreboding settled over the clearing.

"I am well aware of who I am," Auzrael replied evenly, his voice steady despite the undercurrent of tension. "I do not need you to remind me of my duties."

Behomath's words continued, each syllable a warning that hung heavy in the air. "You cannot remain here, Auzrael. Tomorrow morning, you must return to Hell. You are to be crowned Prince, and your father's ambitions leave no room for sentiment."

Auzrael's gaze shifted, his eyes meeting Elvira's momentarily before returning to Behomath. The realization of his impending departure seemed to cast a shadow over the newfound connection he had forged in the mortal realm.

Behomath's voice was stern, a reminder of the harsh reality that awaited. "She cannot be your concern, Auzrael. Your compassion towards this human could lead to dire consequences. Your father's wrath is not to be taken lightly."

Auzrael's jaw clenched, the conflict within him palpable. He tore his gaze away from Elvira and Alvin, his eyes locking onto the Behomath. "I have not forgotten my purpose," he retorted, his tone resolute. "But I also recognize the value of compassion, of protecting those who cannot defend themselves."

The Behomath's gaze bore into Auzrael's, a silent battle of wills playing out beneath the moon's watchful gaze. "Compassion can be a double-edged sword," he cautioned, his voice a cautionary murmur. "Remember what happened to those who dared defy their true nature."

Auzrael's gaze hardened, his fiery eyes narrowing as the weight of the demon's warning settled upon him. In that moment, he stood at a crossroads—between the duty he had sworn to uphold and the stirring of something unfamiliar and unsettling within his heart.

As the night breeze rustled through the trees, Auzrael's gaze returned to Elvira, who cradled Alvin with a tenderness that spoke of a love that transcended the boundaries of their worlds. The demon's expression softened, a mixture of determination and uncertainty etched across his features.

Auzrael's resolve solidified, his internal struggle giving way to a firm determination. He straightened his posture, his gaze fixed unwaveringly on Behomath, and his voice carried a commanding edge that echoed his princely status.

"Behomath," he intoned, his tone authoritative, "I command you not to speak of this encounter to anyone, be it demon or mortal. This is a matter that concerns only us."

Behomath's gaze met Auzrael's, his own demeanor a mix of acknowledgment and compliance. "As you command, Prince Auzrael," he responded, a subtle dip of his head indicating his acceptance of the directive.

Auzrael's grip on his emotions remained resolute as he continued, "Now leave us be and return to your realm. There is no need for further interference."

Behomath turned to depart, his retreating figure a silent testament to the complex dynamics that governed their world. Just before he vanished from view, he cast a lingering look back at Auzrael, his expression one of understanding and empathy.

"Az, I speak as friend not as a member of the court," Behomath's voice carried a note of genuine concern, "that as you navigate this path, the weight of your decisions is your burden to bear. May you find the strength to do what is right, not just as a prince, but as a man."

With those parting words, Behomath disappeared into the shadows, leaving Auzrael and Elvira once again alone in the moonlit clearing.

Auzrael's gaze returned to Elvira, his expression a mix of turmoil and determination. He approached her, his presence a reassuring anchor amidst the whirlwind of emotions that surrounded them.

As the moon hung like a silver crescent in the night sky, casting its gentle glow upon their intertwined fates, Auzrael extended his hand towards Elvira. "Come, Elvira," he said softly, his voice a mixture of sadness and resolve. "We have but a few remaining hours. Let us make the most of them."

Taking his hand, Elvira met his gaze, her own eyes shimmering with unspoken emotions. As they walked together through the moonlit woods, their steps a silent echo of the choices and challenges that lay ahead, the bond between them deepened—a connection forged not only by destiny, but by the shared understanding of the complexities of love, duty, and the timeless dance between the mortal and the supernatural.

Chapter 9

E lvira's POV

Elvira's peaceful slumber is suddenly shattered by the arrival of a haunting nightmare. She tosses and turns in her bed, her face contorted with fear. In the dream, she finds herself trapped in a dimly lit room, shadows dancing menacingly along the walls.

A sinister voice whispers into her ear, "You can't escape, Elvira..."

My eyes dart around the room, I could hear my heart racing.

Another voice mocks her, "Your fears have caught up to you..."

Sweat beads form on my forehead as my breathing becomes rapid and shallow. I let out a trembling gasp.

Whispering to myself, "No, this isn't real... I have to wake up..."

The room seems to close in around me, the walls pressing closer and closer. Panic rises within me like a tidal wave.

The voice mocks me again, "You thought you could hide from me?"

Tears well up in my eyes as I struggle against the suffocating grip of the nightmare.

As I battled the nightmare's grip, Auzrael's footsteps paused momentarily. He looked towards the window, a faint concern etching onto his features. As the nightmare started to lose its grip, Auzrael's instincts sensed my distress. With sudden urgency, he halted his patrol and swiftly made his way to my side. The moonlight filtering through the curtains cast a gentle glow on my troubled features. His hand reached out, fingers brushing against my cheek in a soothing caress. His touch was tender yet strong, a silent reassurance that I was not alone.

Auzrael whispered softly, "Elvira, it's alright. You're safe." My eyes fluttered open, breathing gradually returning to normal. The remnants of the nightmare still lingered, but Auzrael's presence brought a comforting anchor to reality.

My heart still raced from the remnants of the nightmare, yet a newfound sense of courage coursed through my veins. With gratitude and an overwhelming rush of emotions, I gazed into Auzrael's eyes, my lips parting slightly as if to speak my unspoken feelings.

In that charged moment, I closed the distance between us, lips softly brushing against Auzrael's in a gentle and tentative kiss. His initial surprise quickly transformed into a stillness that spread through his entire being.

I pulled back slightly, searching Auzrael's eyes for a response. However, his expression was locked in a frozen state, features almost statue-like. The weight of his unresponsive posture fell heavily upon me, my heart sinking with a mix of confusion and hurt.

My voice trembled as I called out, "Auzrael...?" His silence was deafening, and my mind raced to interpret the sudden change in his demeanor. Doubt crept into my thoughts, vulnerability compounded by the possibility of rejection.

My lips trembled, eyes glistening with unshed tears. I took a step back, my body language betraying the emotional turmoil I was experiencing. "I'm sorry... I didn't mean to... I thought..." Without another word, he closed the gap between us, his lips meeting mine in a kiss that caught me off guard. He cupped my cheek and pulled me into his arms.

I run my fingers through the soft red velvet blankets and matching cushions. Grabbing the blanket, I try to cover myself so he doesn't see how hard I'm squeezing my legs together or just how obvious my nipples are at the sight of him. The space between my legs grows damp, and it only gets worse when he stares intensely into my eyes. A predator that has finally cornered his prey. A demon that has finally found a soul. Goosebumps pebble along my skin, but not from the cold. Even though I can't see his face, he's looks at me like he's going to devour me, lick and bite every inch and not leave a single crumb.

He stops and cocks his head. I blink, momentarily transfixed at the sight of his body from his nearness. I shake my head. I have to tear my eyes away from the hard muscles of his body and candles beside my bed. There's almost an otherworldly hue to it. "Is this a dream?"

"No."

He's lying. This must be a dream.

The bed dips when he leans forward, placing his weight on his hands pressed flat on either side of the bed. Every inch of him is hypnotic, not just because of the smoke dancing on his skin, but because he's sculpted like a Greek god.

He grabs my wrists and holds them above my head with a single hand. The combination of the two moves has a whimper escaping my throat. I swear somehow the shadows beneath his hood darken.

"This is just a dream," I say to myself, rather than him.

"Tell me, my love." He drags his free hand from my ankle, up my thigh and to my hip, slowly, ever so slowly, holding it down when I try to shift away from him. Then he moves his hand between my legs.

I buckle when a whisper of a touch slithers over my lips, making me feel like this is definitely real. "Do you often dream of me between your legs?" As if his soul is pulling away from his body, a dark shadow forms behind him, growing in size and unfurling like a true creature of the night.

I try to move away as the shadow develops a mind of its own, reaching for my throat and wrapping its cool fingers around it. The pressure doesn't hurt, but it starts a deep pulse between my legs as—he—steals my breath.

He grazes my glistening heat as a low growl starts in his throat. Then he drags his hand beneath the robe over the soft skin of my stomach to grab a full breast.

I'm too breathless to respond, not for the lack of air, but for the way he assaults my nipple. Twisting and pinching ruthlessly

I whimper and buck my hips up, trying to gain some friction. I feel so pathetic, having a dirty dream about a man I barely know. I moan, not recognizing this desperate person that I am, wanting his skin on mine and to be full of everything he wants me to feel. It has been so long since I've been touched. I need his touch, too.

"Do you want me to stop? Still think it's a dream?" He asks cockily.

"No," I choke out.

"Do not move your hands from this spot, or you will learn just how monstrous I can be. Do you understand?"

The pressure around my throat increases and his hands move to the next nipple, abusing it as he did the other. "Nod your head if you understand."

I nod. He leans down, blinding me with the darkness beneath his hood. My back arches involuntarily when his chest caresses my nipples. He pulls my bottom lip between his teeth sharply and my breath stutters. He licks the wound and pulls away, letting go of my throat.

"Good girl."

The shadowed hands fondle with my breast, giving them more attention than they've ever received in their life.

"What are you doing?" I pant when he lowers himself until my heat is in the same line of sight as his eyes.

"I cooked meals for you for almost two weeks. It's only fair that you offer me one in return." He draws a single finger over my clit, then pushes into my entrance and hisses. "So beautiful."

I cry out from the combined stimulation of the shadowed hands and his real one. "I can smell your need for me, El. I have made a decision, do you want to know what it is?"

It takes everything in me not to tell him to add another finger and just let me fall off the edge of bliss. His fingers kept moving in and out of me, curling slightly to hit the spot that would make me see stars. But his lazy motions tell me he's not even trying.

I forget that he asked me something until a shadowed hand slaps my breast. "Your words, love."

My brain is in too much of a frenzy to think of what it might be. "Yes."

"I'm not just going to taste you. I'm going to hear you scream."

A nun would go red with his words. "What—"

I swallow my words when another finger is shoved inside of me, and everything around me stops existing. There is only him and the swirls moving across his chest. I don't get a chance to compose myself before he drops his head and starts lapping at my clit like a starved man who has just received his first meal. "Fuck," he snarls, and it's almost like he's laughing to himself in disbelief as a needy moan leaves my lips when he takes me in between his teeth. "I am going to devour you."

I try to squeeze my legs and am met with a sharp assault to the side of my ass before he grabs the flesh like a lifeline, dulling the pain.

His fingers curl, and I do exactly what he said; I scream. I don't even hear his growls of approval as he continues repeating the motion, flicking his tongue faster and faster, like I will run away any second.

Auzrael's hand grips my thigh with his free hand hard enough to leave an imprint on my skin that will bruise come morning. "Sing for me, my love," he whispers against my skin as he curls his fingers and hits the part of me that I forgot existed.

I scream his name out like a banshee, and buck my hips. Unbridled ecstasy rips through every inch of me. He continues with his feast, sucking and licking until there is nothing left for me to give him, my body and mind going limp with the pleasure I have been starved of. "Oh, my love," he mumbles against the inside of my thigh, grazing his lips along the soft skin before biting down, leaving small marks along my skin. "Oh, my little Sphinx. You are a dream. Nothing could compare to the taste of you."

Heat flushes my cheeks at the compliment. I have never felt so satisfied. He removes his fingers from me, I grip his arm, "please, fuck me." I beg him.

He presses his soft lips to mine, and the smell of morning dew and a summer's breeze wafts over me, dissolving my doubts. His warm breath fans the shell of my ear as he says, "I have longed for the taste of you, and now that I have it, I will never know another. When I fuck you, there won't be any candles. It won't be to ease your pain. When I claim you, it will be on my terms. But it will not be tonight."

I let a whimper escape my lips, after being left high and dry. He can't seriously just leave me a wet and needy mess and deny me the simple pleasure of a second orgasm.

"Please," I whisper, grinding my hips into the bed to reach another release. "Please?"

"Please, Az. I want to come again," I beg, voice low and meek. He does nothing for a moment, then he finally leans in and kisses me. It isn't hungry or demanding, isn't filled with lust or need. The kiss is one of silent understanding and mutual connection, but also like he's proud of me. Then he pulls away. Before I can blink, I'm thrown onto my hands and knees.

"You will be the death of me, human." He growls in my ear.

A thick finger slides through my wet heat, then pushes into me. I throw my head back and groan, my eyes automatically rolling to the back of my head. Az takes the opening as a chance to grip my hair to force me to look up at him.

I grind my hips, drawing pleasure from the shadow as his finger slams into me.

I'm whimpering and mewling, teetering on the edge of release, when the shadow's pumps slow, though the hold on my hips doesn't falter. "Relax, my love. I'm not done with you yet." I frown, only to scream when another finger pushes into my pussy, stretching it to the point of agony. Tears of both pain and pleasure pricks my eyes. It's larger than anything I have ever been with.

Movement just below my line of sight catches my attention. I try to move my head but his grip in my hair stops me from getting far. "What are you doing?" I gasp, biting my lip as I pant and try to hold back another scream. I swear I see a sinister smile flash across his face. "It's only fair that you taste me too." My eyes widen before my head is pushed straight down onto his cock. My mouth barely fits around him, still he pushes further inside me. He doesn't make it far before I gag, but he doesn't relent, the sound not a deterrent but an encouragement.

"All of it. Just like I told you to." His voice is firm, not revealing if he feels as undone by me as I am by him.

When I can't take it anymore, my hands and knees collapse beneath me. I'm writhing and trembling, trying to take my fill of the explosion of bliss caused by the unknown and his shadow, all while they keep me upright with their continued assault. He releases himself into my mouth. I try to take every sweet drop of him and swallow, laving at every inch of him with my tongue. "You were more amazing than anything I could have imagined, my little sphinx."

He dips beside me, taking me into embrace and I snuggle closer to him. "Don't leave me." I whisper to him. I don't hear any movement from him, I close my eyes and this time I dreamt of nothing.

Chapter 10

The morning sun began to paint the sky with hues of gold and rose, casting a warm glow over the clearing where Auzrael, Elvira, and Alvin had shared their brief respite. As the first rays of light filtered through the trees, a sense of quiet anticipation hung in the air—a reminder that the inevitable moment of parting had arrived.

Unbeknownst to Elvira, Auzrael stood near the edge of the clearing, his eyes fixed upon her as she cradled Alvin in her arms, the innocence of their bond a bittersweet tableau that tugged at his heart. His decision to leave was a heavy one, born of the complex interplay between his responsibilities as a prince and the newfound connection he had forged.

With a heavy sigh, Auzrael turned away, his footsteps soundless as he moved toward the forest's edge. He knew that his absence would be felt, but he also recognized the importance of his role in the demon realm—an intricate web of power and politics that demanded his attention.

As he disappeared into the embrace of the woods, he left behind a folded piece of parchment, carefully placed where Elvira would find it. The note bore his distinct script, a testament to the careful consideration that had gone into his words:

Elvira,

Though our time together was brief, it was a gift I will forever hold close to my heart.

Know that I leave not out of choice, but out of necessity, a duty I cannot ignore. But should you ever find yourself in dire need, should the shadows of danger darken your path, know that you need only call upon my name, and I will come.

The map to the fae is on the table.

Until our paths cross again,

Auzrael

As Auzrael vanished into the depths of the forest, his absence was felt like a whisper in the wind—a departure marked by the weight of unspoken emotions and the promise of a future that remained uncertain.

The morning sun cast a soft glow upon the clearing, illuminating the space where Auzrael had stood just hours before. Elvira, her heart heavy with a sense of longing and unease, ventured to the edge of the clearing. Her gaze fell upon a folded piece of parchment, its presence drawing her attention like a magnet.

As she picked up the parchment and unfolded it, Auzrael's familiar script came into view, his words etched upon the page like a bittersweet melody. The letter held a promise and a farewell, a declaration of a bond that had touched her soul in ways she could scarcely comprehend.

Elvira's heart felt as though it had been torn in two as she read Auzrael's letter. The weight of his absence bore down on her like a heavy stone, and her tears fell freely, staining the parchment with the evidence of her grief. The emotions that had surged between them, the intimacy they had shared, now felt like fragile memories slipping through her fingers.

Her fingers trembled as she traced the words on the page, her mind replaying the night before—the tenderness, the passion, and the connection that had seemed so profound. And yet, he had left without a word, without an explanation, leaving her to grapple with a whirlwind of emotions that ranged from longing to confusion.

"Auzrael," she choked out his name, her voice a mixture of sorrow and a longing she could barely put into words. She clutched the letter to her chest, as if trying to hold onto the memory of his touch, the sound of his voice, and the warmth of his presence.

Alvin, sensing Elvira's distress, reached out his tiny hand and touched her cheek, his innocent gaze filled with concern. Elvira's tears fell onto his hand, and she looked down at him, her heart breaking and mending all at once.

"He's gone, Alvin," she whispered, her voice cracking. "He left without a word, and I don't know why."

As she held her baby close, Elvira's tears continued to flow, her sobs echoing in the quiet of the forest. The night they had shared, so filled with promise and intimacy, now felt like a distant dream, overshadowed by the reality of Auzrael's departure.

"Why did you leave, Auzrael?" she cried out to the empty air, her words carried away by the wind. "Why didn't you say anything?"

The ache in her heart seemed almost unbearable, a mixture of love and loss that left her feeling adrift in a sea of emotions. The memory of their night together was a delicate ember, threatened to be extinguished by the uncertainty of his absence.

With a heavy sigh, Elvira pressed the letter to her lips, a silent kiss that carried the weight of her feelings. She knew that Auzrael's departure was not a rejection, but the pain of his absence cut deep nonetheless. Clinging to the promise he had left, the assurance of his help when needed, she whispered to herself, "I'll hold onto this, Auzrael. Until the day we meet again."

With Auzrael's promise echoing in her heart, Elvira knew that she couldn't let her grief consume her. The path ahead was uncertain, but she had a purpose—to protect Alvin and to find a way to navigate the challenges that lay before them.

Gathering her belongings and cradling Alvin close, Elvira set out on a journey that would take them to the realm of the fae. She had heard whispers of their ethereal beauty and their powerful magic—a world that seemed like a distant dream compared to the darkness they had faced.

The journey was long and filled with its own trials, but fueled by determination and a newfound strength, Elvira pressed on. She navigated through enchanted forests, crossed shimmering rivers, and followed the guidance of whispered winds that seemed to carry the promise of the fae realm.

Finally, after what felt like an eternity of travel, the landscape around them began to shift. The air grew charged with a palpable energy, and a sense of otherworldly beauty enveloped them. Trees glowed with a soft luminescence, flowers danced in vibrant hues, and the very air seemed to hum with magic.

As they ventured deeper into this mystical realm, they came upon a clearing bathed in a radiant light. Before them stood a trio of fae, their presence exuding an aura of regality and grace. Their wings shimmered like the delicate gossamer of dreams, and their eyes held a depth of wisdom that spoke of ages gone by.

Elvira's journey led her to the mystical realm of the fae, a realm of enchantment and ethereal beauty that seemed worlds away from the darkness she had known. With Alvin cradled protectively in her arms, she stepped into the heart of the fae court, her heart fluttering with a mixture of hope and trepidation.

The fae court was a breathtaking tableau of otherworldly splendor, its inhabitants radiating an air of elegance and magic. Elvira's presence drew curious glances and hushed whispers, her status as a human in their midst a testament to the rarity of her presence.

As she approached the heart of the court, Elvira's gaze fell upon the royal fae—an elegant figure adorned in resplendent attire, a crown of starlight resting upon her brow. This was the queen, the ruler of the fae realm, a being whose power seemed to resonate with the very essence of the land.

With a mixture of determination and deference, Elvira stepped forward, her voice clear yet respectful. "I have come seeking your wisdom and guidance, Your Highness," she began, her words carrying a weight that extended beyond their spoken syllables. "This child," she continued, her gaze tenderly fixated on Alvin, "belongs to a lineage of both werewolf and fae."

A ripple of curiosity swept through the fae court as Elvira's words hung in the air. Whispers of intrigue and uncertainty fluttered among the gathered fae, their attention fixated on the human woman who dared to stand before their queen.

The royal fae regarded Elvira with a mixture of curiosity and calculation, her eyes seeming to penetrate beyond the surface and into the very heart of her intentions. Moments passed, the silence stretching as the court awaited the queen's response.

Then, a trio of fae stepped forward, their expressions disdainful and their voices dripping with condescension. "A hybrid child," one of them sneered, his tone laced with scorn. "A disgrace to the purity of our realm."

Elvira's heart sank at their words, a mixture of anger and desperation surging within her. She had braved the unknown, crossed realms, and faced countless challenges to ensure Alvin's safety, only to be met with rejection and prejudice.

But just as her hope threatened to dim, a commanding voice cut through the air, its authority undeniable. "Enough." The single word, spoken by the royal fae herself, silenced the dissenting voices and quelled the murmurs that had begun to rise.

The queen's gaze shifted from her subjects to Elvira, a hint of recognition flickering in her eyes. "Step forward, child," she beckoned, her tone a blend of grace and command.

With a mixture of trepidation and curiosity, Elvira obeyed, approaching the queen with Alvin held securely in her arms. The queen's scrutinizing gaze seemed to linger on the baby, her expression thoughtful and her eyes narrowing as if searching for something hidden beneath the surface.

And then, in a moment that seemed to stretch beyond time itself, recognition dawned upon the queen's features—a realization that seemed to electrify the air. "This child," she spoke, her voice carrying a sense of awe and wonder, "bears the blood of our realm."

A hush fell over the fae court, a collective gasp of astonishment and reverence rippling through the gathered crowd. Elvira's heart raced as she absorbed the weight of the queen's words, her gaze flickering between the ruler of the fae and the baby in her arms.

The queen extended a hand, her gesture a blend of invitation and acceptance. "Give him to me."

With a mixture of hope and uncertainty, Elvira carefully placed Alvin into the queen's awaiting arms. The baby's innocent gaze met the fae ruler's, and in that poignant exchange, a profound connection seemed to form—a recognition that transcended both realms and bound them together in ways none could have foreseen.

As the queen cradled Alvin close, her expression softened into one of tenderness and protectiveness. "He is of our bloodline," she declared, her voice carrying the weight of authority. "He is my grandson, a child of the fae."

The air shifted then, the queen then questioned, "Where is my daughter?"

Elvira's heart clenched as the weight of the queen's question settled upon her shoulders. The air seemed to still, the anticipation of her response hanging palpably in the air. She met the queen's gaze, her eyes brimming with sorrow and a quiet resolve.

"Your Highness," Elvira began, her voice steady yet tinged with the unmistakable undercurrent of grief. "Your daughter... Alvin's mother... she is no longer with us." The words hung heavily in the air, a somber acknowledgment of the pain that had shaped their shared journey.

A ripple of sorrow swept through the fae court, a collective gasp of realization echoing among the gathered fae. The queen's expression remained inscrutable, her gaze fixed upon Elvira as if seeking to unravel the truth that lay beneath her words.

Elvira continued, her voice soft yet resolute. "She gave her life to protect Alvin and ensure his safety. Alongside my parents, they faced a great threat—a darkness that sought to consume them both. Their sacrifice was immense, a testament to the love and bravery that flowed through their veins."

The fae court seemed to hold its breath, the weight of the revelation settling like a heavy shroud over the gathered beings. The sorrow in Elvira's voice was palpable, her words a haunting reminder of the sacrifices that had been made to ensure Alvin's survival.

The queen's features remained composed, but a glimmer of emotion danced within her eyes—a mixture of pain, understanding, and perhaps even a touch of regret. "My daughter..." she whispered, her voice carrying a sense of melancholy and a hint of a mother's longing.

Elvira's gaze softened as she met the queen's eyes. "She was brave," she said, her words a tribute to the fallen fae. "And her love for Alvin was unwavering. She gave everything to protect him, to give him a chance at life."

The queen's arms tightened around Alvin, the baby nestled against her with an almost instinctual closeness. In that poignant moment, a silent understanding seemed to pass between the human and the fae—a shared recognition of the bond that had connected their lives, and the sacrifices that had paved the way for their present circumstances.

With a gentle nod, the queen turned her attention back to Elvira, her gaze a mix of gratitude and a sense of closure. "You have brought my grandson back to where he rightfully belongs," she said, her voice carrying a note of solemnity. "Your journey has been one of hardship and determination, and for that, you have my thanks."

She turned to the advisor, "Give the girl a room in the east wing and make sure she is not displeased with our services."

Tears welled in Elvira's eyes as she met the queen's gaze, a mixture of emotions swirling within her—sorrow for the loss of her parents, gratitude for the acceptance she had found in the fae realm, and a sense of fulfillment that her mission had been fulfilled.

Within the ethereal realm of the royal fae court, a sense of purpose and urgency filled the air. Elvira stood amidst the majestic beings, her presence a testament to the unbreakable bond that had formed between the human and fae realms. The memory of her journey, the sacrifices made, and the connection she had forged with Alvin had woven her into the very fabric of their destiny.

Queen Amalthea, her regal presence commanding the attention of all, addressed the assembly. Her voice carried a blend of authority and determination, resonating through the ornate chamber. "The time has come for us to confront the source of the darkness that has plagued both our worlds," she declared, her gaze sweeping over the gathered fae. "The evil witch who seeks to tear apart the veil between the supernatural realm and the human realm must be stopped."

Murmurs of agreement rippled through the fae court, their expressions a mixture of resolve and concern. The witch's malevolent actions had cast a shadow over their realms, threatening the delicate balance that had been maintained for centuries.

Elvira's heart raced as she listened to the queen's words. She had braved challenges, faced demons, and journeyed across realms, all to protect Alvin and mend the tear that had sundered their worlds. Now, the prospect of confronting the very source of their strife filled her with a sense of purpose and a determination to see their mission through to the end.

Queen Amalthea turned her attention to Elvira, her gaze holding a mixture of gratitude and empathy. "You have walked the path between our worlds, young one," she said, her voice softening. "Your courage and determination have brought us together. We ask for your aid in this endeavor."

Elvira met the queen's eyes, her resolve unyielding. "I will do whatever it takes to ensure that the darkness is vanquished," she replied, her voice carrying a steely determination. "Alvin's future, the safety of both our realms—they are worth any sacrifice."

The queen nodded, her approval evident. "Very well. We shall forge a plan to confront the witch and restore the balance."

As the fae court convened, strategies were discussed, alliances formed, and the intricate threads of a plan began to weave together. Elvira's insights, drawn from her experiences in the human realm, were invaluable, offering a unique perspective that contributed to the collective strategy.

In the days that followed, Elvira found herself immersed in preparations. Potions were brewed, spells were cast, and weapons were forged—each element a vital piece of the puzzle that would lead them to their confrontation with the witch.

The day of reckoning arrived, the air charged with a mixture of tension and determination. Elvira stood among the fae warriors, her heart a steady drumbeat of anticipation. She had chosen not to accompany them into battle, instead entrusting her companions with the task of confronting the witch directly. Her place was with Alvin, ensuring his safety and awaiting their return.

As the fae warriors departed, Elvira's gaze lingered on the horizon, her thoughts a tapestry of hope, anxiety, and a quiet resolve. She held onto the memory of her journey, the people she had met, and the strength that had been forged through hardship.

Hours turned into an agonizing wait, time stretching like an eternity. With Alvin nestled in her arms, Elvira paced the chamber, her ears attuned to the echoes of the battle beyond. Her heart ached with every passing moment, her thoughts consumed by the well-being of her fae companions.

And then, as the sun dipped below the horizon and the first hints of starlight emerged, a ripple of energy swept through the room. The air seemed to shift, carrying with it a sense of triumph and relief.

The fae warriors returned, their expressions a mixture of weariness and satisfaction. Elvira's gaze locked onto their leader, a sense of anticipation coursing through her veins. Queen Amalthea stepped forward, her eyes meeting Elvira's with a mix of gravity and triumph.

"The witch has been defeated," the queen announced, her voice carrying the weight of their victory. "The tear between our realms has been mended."

Tears welled in Elvira's eyes, a surge of emotions coursing through her. Relief, joy, and an overwhelming sense of accomplishment washed over her, their intensity nearly overwhelming.

The fae warriors approached, their gazes filled with respect and admiration. "Your aid was instrumental in our victory," their leader said, his voice carrying a note of gratitude.

Elvira nodded, her heart swelling with a mixture of humility and pride. "We did this together," she replied, her voice steady. "For Alvin, for our realms, for the future."

In that moment, as the fae court stood united, a sense of unity and purpose seemed to transcend the boundaries that had once divided them. The darkness that had threatened to engulf their worlds had been vanquished, replaced by a renewed sense of hope and the promise of a future where the supernatural and human realms could coexist in harmony.

As Elvira held Alvin close, her heart full of gratitude, she knew that their journey was far from over. But together, with the bonds they had formed and the strength they had discovered, they were prepared to face whatever challenges lay ahead—knowing that their connection, like the tapestry of their shared destiny, was unbreakable.

7 months later,

Seven months had passed since the victorious battle against the evil witch, and the fae realm had begun to heal. The once-torn fabric between the supernatural and human realms had been meticulously woven back together, allowing a fragile sense of harmony to blossom. Within the heart of the fae court, Elvira and Alvin had found a new home, a place where they were welcomed and embraced by those who recognized the resilience and courage that had brought them there.

In a sunlit glade, adorned with flowers that seemed to shimmer with otherworldly hues, Elvira knelt beside Alvin. The infant had grown, his features a delightful blend of his fae heritage and the werewolf lineage that had been woven into his very existence. His laughter, like tinkling bells, filled the air as he reached out to grasp a delicate blossom.

"Careful, little one," Elvira cooed, her voice a soothing melody. "We don't want to hurt the flowers."

Alvin's bright eyes sparkled with innocent curiosity, his fingers brushing against the petals as he giggled. It was a moment of pure joy, a testament to the simple pleasures that life within the fae realm had brought them.

As they played, the fae court observed from a respectful distance, their expressions a mixture of awe and acceptance. While some remnants of prejudice still lingered, the bond that had formed between Elvira and Alvin had slowly begun to erode those barriers, allowing understanding and compassion to take root.

In a burst of delight, Alvin's tiny hand closed around a petal, and he tugged it free from the stem. His laughter filled the glade as he proudly held up his prize, his eyes alight with triumph.

"Good job, Alvin," Elvira praised, her heart swelling with affection. "You're quite the little adventurer, aren't you?"

As Alvin basked in his victory, his gaze shifted from the flower to Elvira, his expression one of anticipation and delight. And then, in a moment that seemed to hang suspended in time, his lips formed the shapes of his first words.

"Vira," he uttered, his voice a melodic whisper that sent a shiver of emotion down Elvira's spine.

Tears gathered in Elvira's eyes as she met Alvin's gaze, her heart overflowing with a mixture of love and gratitude. "Yes, my sweet Alvin," she replied, her voice soft and filled with tenderness. "I'm here."

Alvin's laughter bubbled forth once more, his eyes crinkling at the corners as he basked in the joy of their connection. But he wasn't done yet. With a sense of determination, he turned his gaze toward the fae court, his tiny hand pointing in the direction of his admirers.

"Mamma," he pronounced, the word a fragile yet powerful declaration that seemed to reverberate through the glade.

A collective gasp swept through the fae court, their astonishment mingling with a sense of wonder. The child's first word was a testament to the profound bond that had formed between Elvira and Alvin—a bond that transcended bloodlines and defied the limitations of prejudice.

Tears streamed down Elvira's cheeks as she held Alvin close, her heart a symphony of emotions that swelled within her chest. "Yes, my precious Alvin," she whispered, her voice choked with emotion. "Thank you for this gift, for being your mamma."

In that poignant moment, the glade seemed to come alive with a sense of magic—an enchantment woven not from spells or potions, but from the purity of love and the resilience of the human spirit.

As the sun bathed the glade in a golden glow, Elvira and Alvin shared a moment of connection that transcended words. In the presence of the fae realm and the echoes of a shared journey, they found a sense of belonging, acceptance, and a future that held the promise of endless possibilities.

And so, amidst the beauty of the fae realm and the echoes of their intertwined destinies, Elvira and Alvin continued to play, their laughter and love a testament to the unbreakable bonds that had shaped their extraordinary tale.

Chapter 11

The day had begun like any other, the sun casting its gentle rays upon the fae realm as life flowed in an intricate dance of beauty and magic. Elvira and Alvin had shared a moment of laughter and playfulness beneath the canopy of trees, the echoes of their connection reverberating through the air. But as the day wore on, a sense of unease began to weave its way through the glade.

It was in the soft glow of twilight that Queen Amalthea approached Elvira, her presence commanding attention. A solemn gravity seemed to hang about her, her expression a mixture of sorrow and purpose. Beside her stood a figure that Elvira had never seen before—a fae woman with an otherworldly aura, her features delicate yet ethereal.

"Elvira," the queen began, her voice carrying a weight that seemed to reverberate through the very air, "there is a fae ceremony, one of great significance and importance. It is an event that only those of fae lineage can attend."

Elvira's heart clenched with a mixture of apprehension and confusion. She held Alvin a little closer, her gaze shifting between the queen and the mysterious fae woman. "But... what does that mean for Alvin?" she asked, a sense of foreboding settling in her chest.

The queen's gaze softened, empathy shining within her eyes. "Fear not, dear Elvira. Alvin will be safe in our care during the ceremony," she reassured, her words carrying a sense of sincerity.

Reluctantly, Elvira handed Alvin over to the queen, her heart aching with the weight of separation. "Promise me he'll be well taken care of," she implored, her voice tinged with both hope and trepidation.

"We give you our word," the queen replied, her tone gentle yet resolute.

As the queen and the mysterious fae woman departed, Alvin cradled in the queen's arms, Elvira's gaze remained fixed on their retreating figures. She felt a mixture of longing and uncertainty, a feeling that was only amplified by the impending ceremony that loomed on the horizon.

Hours passed, each minute feeling like an eternity as Elvira's anticipation mingled with a sense of impending dread. And then, as the stars emerged in a tapestry of shimmering light, the queen returned. Beside her stood a figure that sent a jolt of shock through Elvira's veins—a fae woman, radiant and otherworldly, her presence seeming almost too beautiful to be real. It was the girl that her father had brought, the one is supposed to be dead.

What more worried her was the absence of Alvin in the queen's arms. Her heart pounded in her chest, a rising tide of panic threatening to engulf her.

"Elvira," the queen's voice was gentle, a balm to her frayed nerves. "I would like you to meet my daughter, Aine."

"Where is Alvin?" She gritted out, "your majesty."

"You know that Aine was lost to us, taken by the clutches of death," the queen continued, her voice carrying a sense of sorrow and hope intertwined. "But through a rare and ancient fae ritual that was found in the witch's books, we were able to bring her back from the realm beyond."

Elvira's breath caught in her throat, her mind struggling to comprehend the implications of the queen's words. Aine had returned from the dead—brought back through a fae ritual that surely held immense power and consequence.

"But..." Elvira's voice trembled, her gaze darting between the queen and Aine. "Where is Alvin?"

The queen's expression softened, a mixture of understanding and sympathy emanating from her. "To bring Aine back from the realm of the departed, a sacrifice had to be made. A life for a life."

The weight of the truth settled upon Elvira like a heavy stone. Her heart seemed to shatter within her chest, the realization hitting her with a force that left her breathless. Alvin, her precious Alvin, had been the sacrifice.

Tears welled in Elvira's eyes as she struggled to find her voice, her grief and anguish a tumultuous tempest within her. "No..." she whispered, the word a fragile plea that carried the weight of a mother's devastation.

Aine stepped forward, her gaze filled with a mixture of gratitude and sorrow. "I understand the pain this has caused you, Elvira," she said, her voice carrying a sense of empathy that cut through the sea of emotions. "For that, I am truly sorry."

Aine's words hung in the air, a fragile bridge between two hearts weighed down by the burden of sorrow and sacrifice. Her voice carried the weight of genuine remorse, an attempt to bridge the chasm of loss that had opened between them.

But as Aine stepped forward, her expression filled with a mixture of empathy and apology, Elvira's anger simmered beneath the surface. The sea of emotions within her roiled and churned, and her chest tightened with a mixture of grief and fury.

"You understand?" Elvira's voice trembled, the edges of her words sharp with bitterness. "You understand nothing about the pain I'm feeling."

Aine's eyes widened, her features a canvas of surprise and realization. The depth of Elvira's anguish, the searing ache of a mother who had lost her child, seemed to cut through the veil of Aine's own experiences.

Elvira's voice cracked as her anger surged to the forefront, raw and unfiltered. "Alvin was more than just a son to me," she spat, her words a torrent of emotions that she could no longer contain. "He was my light, my hope, the reason I fought through every trial and tribulation. And now you tell me he's gone? Sacrificed?"

Aine's gaze wavered, her own sorrow mingling with a growing understanding of the magnitude of her actions. "Elvira, I never meant—"

"You never meant?" Elvira's laughter was tinged with bitterness, a bitter echo of the joy that had once filled her heart. "You tampered with forces beyond your control, and now you've taken the one thing that meant everything to me."

Tears streamed down Elvira's cheeks, her pain a tangible force that seemed to reverberate through the glade. Her voice rose to a scream, a primal expression of the anguish that threatened to consume her. "What right did you have? What right to play with his life?"

Aine's own tears glistened as she reached out, her hand trembling as if attempting to bridge the vast chasm between them. "Elvira, I was lost in my grief. I wanted my daughter back, but I never understood the depth of your bond with Alvin."

Elvira's gaze seethed with a mixture of fury and anguish. "Your daughter? Your daughter, Aine, is the reason my Alvin is gone. Do you even comprehend what you've done?"

Aine's shoulders slumped, the weight of the consequences settling heavily upon her. "I thought... I thought I could fix what had been broken. I thought I could bring her back and set things right."

Elvira's chest heaved as she stepped forward, her voice a shattered whisper. "And in doing so, you shattered my world."

The glade seemed to hold its breath, the air thick with the intensity of their emotions. Aine's expression crumpled with remorse, her own pain mirroring Elvira's in a way that transcended their differences.

"I curse you, Aine," Elvira's voice was a venomous hiss, her words infused with the weight of her grief and anger. "May the pain of loss consume you as it has consumed me. May you feel the emptiness of a heart shattered beyond repair."

Aine's tears fell freely as she whispered, her voice a mixture of acceptance and resignation. "I will bear that curse, Elvira, for I deserve it."

Aine's whispered words hung in the air, her voice heavy with the weight of her own remorse. The glade seemed to hold its breath, the tendrils of sorrow and anger intertwining like a delicate dance of emotions. But before the moment could stretch into eternity, the queen stepped forward, her presence a resolute force that seemed to cut through the tension.

"Enough, Aine," the queen's voice was firm, her eyes locking onto Elvira's with a warning that carried the weight of her authority. "Be cautious of what you say, for words spoken in anger can have consequences beyond measure."

Aine's tearful gaze shifted from Elvira to her mother, a mixture of pain and understanding reflected in her eyes. She nodded, her voice silenced by the gravity of the moment.

But Elvira, lost in the depths of her grief and consumed by her anger, paid no heed to the queen's warning. Her heart was a tempest of emotions, her pain a burning fire that refused to be extinguished.

"You deserve it?" Elvira's voice was laced with bitter incredulity, her words a scathing echo of her torment. "You think bearing a curse will absolve you of the pain you've caused?"

The queen's gaze hardened, a sense of protectiveness enveloping her daughter. "Elvira," she admonished, her voice a measured reminder.

But Elvira's resolve seemed unbreakable, her voice rising in a crescendo of grief-fueled anger. "You played with forces you didn't understand. You took my Alvin away, and for what? To satisfy your own desires?"

The queen's patience seemed to wane, her eyes flashing with a mixture of sternness and concern. "I warned you, Elvira. Your words carry weight, and in your grief, you risk consequences you cannot fathom."

Aine reached out to her mother, her touch a plea for understanding. "Mother, please, let us find a way to make amends."

But Elvira's pain had reached a breaking point, her emotions too raw to be contained. "Amends?" she scoffed, her voice a bitter edge to her torment. "Can amends bring back my son? Can they fill the void that now consumes me?"

The queen's expression darkened, her patience exhausted. With a swift motion, she turned to one of her guards and uttered a command. The guard stepped forward, his presence a silent proclamation of authority.

Before Elvira could react, she felt strong hands gripping her arms, pulling her away from Aine and the queen. Her protests fell on deaf ears as the guard's grip tightened, his actions a reflection of the queen's resolve to protect her daughter.

"No! Let me go!" Elvira's voice cracked, her struggles futile against the guard's unyielding strength. Her eyes bore into the queen's, a mixture of betrayal and despair written across her features. "You think throwing me into the dungeons will silence my grief? It won't. Nothing will."

The queen's voice was steady, her gaze unwavering as she met Elvira's eyes. "It is not to silence your grief, but to protect my daughter and our realm from the consequences of your anger."

As Elvira was led away, her heart ached with a sense of injustice and helplessness. The glade, once a place of beauty and magic, had become a prison—a reflection of the pain and fractured bonds that had come to define her journey.

Aine's tearful gaze followed Elvira, a mixture of guilt and sorrow etched onto her features. The queen turned to her daughter, her voice a mix of sternness and concern. "This pain is not hers alone to bear. We must find a way to heal the wounds we have inflicted, before they consume us all."

In the dim, cold depths of the dungeons, Elvira's sobs echoed like a mournful melody, each tear a testament to the overwhelming weight of her grief. Her body trembled with each convulsive breath, her chest heaving as her heart spilled its ache into the darkness.

The chains that bound her to the cold stone wall seemed like a cruel reflection of the chains that bound her heart. Her fingers clenched into fists, her knuckles white with the effort to contain the tempest of emotions that threatened to consume her.

"Why?" Her voice was a broken whisper, a plea that seemed to carry through the damp air. "Why did this have to happen? Why did you take him from me?"

Her cries seemed to merge with the distant echoes of dripping water, the dungeon's eerie symphony a backdrop to her shattered lament. Memories of Alvin's laughter, his innocent smiles, and the warmth of his presence seemed to haunt her, a bittersweet reminder of what had been stolen from her.

She pressed her forehead against the cool stone, her tears mingling with the dampness that clung to the walls. Her body shook with the force of her sobs, her cries a cathartic release of the anguish that had been building within her since the moment she had been torn from him.

"I can't do this... I can't bear this pain," she choked out between sobs, her voice raw with emotion. "He was all I had, all I fought for, and now he's gone."

The darkness seemed to envelop her, a shroud of despair that clung to her like a second skin. She yearned for the light that Alvin had brought into her life, the hope that had sustained her through every trial. Now, that light had been extinguished, leaving her adrift in a sea of darkness.

As the minutes stretched into hours, Elvira's cries began to sub-side, her tears giving way to a weary numbness. She slumped against the wall, her breath ragged and her heart a hollow ache. Her mind was a whirlwind of memories and regrets, a storm that raged within her and threatened to engulf her entirely.

In the midst of her desolation, a glimmer of determination began to emerge. The chains that bound her were not just physical—they were the chains of her grief, her anger, and her pain. And she knew that if she was to honor Alvin's memory, she had to find a way to break free from those chains, to rise above the darkness that threatened to consume her.

With a shaky breath, Elvira lifted her head, her eyes red and puffy from her tears. Elvira's voice quivered as she called out into the darkness, her plea a desperate whisper that seemed to hang in the air.

"Auzrael... please," her voice trembled, the sound a fragile echo of her anguish. "I don't know if you can hear me, but I need you. I need your help."

Her words seemed to merge with the shadows, the dungeon's silence a stark contrast to the turmoil that raged within her. She closed her eyes, her hands gripping the chains that bound her, her fingers white with the intensity of her grip.

"Alvin is gone," she continued, her voice a mixture of grief and desperation. "I couldn't protect him, and now... now I'm trapped here, consumed by my pain."

Tears welled in her eyes, her vision blurred by the haze of her sorrow. She could feel the weight of her words, the raw vulnerability of her plea, hanging in the air around her.

"But I won't give up," her voice grew stronger, a flicker of determination cutting through the darkness. "I won't let this darkness swallow me. I need you, Auzrael. I need your strength, your guidance."

The silence seemed to stretch on, the seconds feeling like an eternity as Elvira waited, her heart pounding in her chest. Her breath hitched, a mixture of hope and fear intertwining within her.

And then, as if in response to her plea, a faint whisper of wind seemed to dance through the dungeon. Elvira's eyes widened, her heart quickening as a presence seemed to materialize in the shadows.

"Elvira," the voice was a soothing murmur, a gentle caress against her turmoil. Auzrael stood before her, his eyes a pool of understanding and compassion.

Tears streamed down Elvira's cheeks as she met his gaze, her voice a mixture of gratitude and longing. "Auzrael... I thought you might not come."

His hand reached out, his touch warm against her cheek. "I told you that I'll always come."

She leaned into his touch, her heart aching with a mixture of emotions. "I don't know what to do," she admitted, her voice a fragile admission of her vulnerability. "I feel so lost, so broken."

Elvira's body trembled uncontrollably, her cries a heart-wrenching symphony that resonated within the depths of Auzrael's being. He held onto her tightly, his arms wrapped around her fragile form as he tried to offer whatever solace he could muster. His touch was gentle yet firm, a silent promise that he was there, unwavering and steadfast.

Resting his hand upon her head, Auzrael's fingers threaded through her hair in a soothing caress. He hoped that his touch, his presence, could convey the unspoken message that she wasn't alone, that he was by her side and would remain there through her darkest hours.

As the moments stretched on, time seemed to be a cruel companion, offering no reprieve from Elvira's anguish. Her cries persisted, a testament to the depth of her pain, and Auzrael held on, his heart aching with a mixture of empathy and a fierce determination to be her anchor in the storm.

The tears continued to flow, each drop a stark reminder of the wounds that marred her soul. Yet, amidst the sea of sorrow, a small gesture of connection emerged. Elvira's trembling hand reached out, her fingers seeking his. Slowly, hesitantly, her hand found his, and their fingers intertwined. It was a fragile bond, a lifeline amidst the tumultuous sea of emotions that threatened to consume them both.

Her grip tightened, her fingers clinging to him as though he were her lifeline. Auzrael felt a mixture of humility and honor, knowing that in this moment, he was her source of strength. Her silent assurance that she would be okay, that she was grateful for his presence, resonated through their touch.

Together, they weathered the storm—Elvira's cries gradually softening, her sobs becoming intermittent. Auzrael held onto her, their connection unbroken, a silent testament to their shared struggle. He knew that the road ahead wouldn't be easy, that her journey through the darkness had just begun. But he believed in her, in her resilience and her capacity to find light even in the bleakest of moments.

As the echoes of her cries began to fade, Auzrael's grip remained steady. He looked down at her, his eyes meeting hers with a mixture of compassion and unwavering support. He whispered no words, for he knew that sometimes, presence spoke louder than any utterance could.

Elvira's eyes, red and swollen from her tears, met his gaze. In that moment, they shared a connection that transcended words—a shared understanding, a promise of solidarity. She was not alone in her pain, and Auzrael was there to be her anchor, her guiding light.

And as they stood there, their fingers intertwined, a quiet determination settled within Elvira's heart. She knew the road ahead would be difficult, but with Auzrael by her side, she felt a glimmer of hope. Together, they would navigate the storm, each step a testament to the strength of their bond and the power of resilience that resided within her.

Chapter 12

Elvira's cries gradually subsided, leaving behind a heavy silence that seemed to hang in the air. Her tear-streaked gaze lifted to meet Auzrael's, a mixture of relief and vulnerability in her eyes. He stood before her, a steadfast presence that had answered her silent call.

As she opened her mouth to speak, to try and convey the whirlwind of emotions and events that had unfolded, Auzrael gently placed a finger against her lips, silencing her words. His expression was a combination of understanding and reassurance, a silent acknowledgment that he already knew the pain she had endured.

"I know," he said softly, his voice carrying a weight of empathy that seemed to bridge the gap between them. "You don't need to explain."

Elvira's heart ached with gratitude for his understanding, for his ability to see beyond her words and into the depths of her soul. She nodded, her gaze never leaving his, a silent exchange of emotions passing between them.

Auzrael's next words were quiet, his voice a mixture of concern and readiness. "Do you want me to take care of this? To remove the ones responsible for your suffering?"

Elvira's immediate instinct was to say yes, to seek vengeance for the pain she had endured. But as she looked into Auzrael's eyes, a deeper understanding seemed to blossom within her. She shook her head slowly, her expression resolute.

"No," her voice was steady, her gaze unwavering. "Killing them won't change what's been done. It won't bring back what I've lost."

Auzrael nodded, a sense of respect and admiration in his eyes. "You're stronger than you know, Elvira."

Her lips quirked into a faint, sad smile. "Maybe I'm learning to be."

Their gaze held, a silent connection that spoke volumes. And then, Elvira's voice softened, her words carrying a vulnerable yearning that seemed to echo from the depths of her heart.

"I don't want revenge, Auzrael," she confessed, her voice barely more than a whisper. "I just want a home. A place where I can heal, where Alvin's memory can live on."

Auzrael's expression softened, a tender understanding passing between them. He reached out, his hand cupping her cheek in a gentle caress.

"You will have that home, Elvira," he vowed, his voice carrying a quiet determination. "I will ensure it."

Tears welled in Elvira's eyes once more, but this time they were tears of hope, of a future that seemed a little less daunting in the presence of the demon who had become her protector, her confidant, and perhaps something more.

Auzrael's proposal hung in the air, a surprising offer that seemed to carry both sincerity and a hint of hope. His gaze remained locked with Elvira's, his expression a mix of earnestness and a longing for her to find a haven amidst the chaos.

"Elvira," his voice was soft, his words carrying a weight of genuine concern. "I can offer you a place in the demon kingdom, a realm where I can ensure your safety. There are humans who live and work there, finding a life amidst the darkness. You could blend in, find a home."

Elvira's heart wavered between uncertainty and the allure of his offer. The thought of a sanctuary, a place where she could heal and rebuild her shattered world, was undeniably tempting. But the idea of dwelling in a realm as foreign and unknown as hell was a daunting prospect.

Her gaze shifted away, her mind a whirlwind of conflicting emotions. "But... wouldn't I be out of place? A human among demons?"

Auzrael's hand gently reached for hers, his touch a reassuring anchor. "You wouldn't be alone, Elvira," he explained, his voice a soothing cadence. "There are humans who have found their way in hell, forging their own paths and lives. You would not be the only one."

Elvira's gaze returned to his, her eyes searching his face for any hint of deception. But all she found was sincerity, a genuine desire to offer her a chance at a new beginning.

"I can protect you there," Auzrael continued, his voice carrying a quiet conviction. "No one would dare trouble you in the demon kingdom. And with time, you might find solace amidst the darkness."

The prospect of a fresh start, of escaping the pain and torment that had plagued her, held a powerful allure. Elvira's heart yearned for healing, for a chance to honor Alvin's memory in a place free from the haunting memories of her past.

Slowly, a small nod of agreement formed on her lips. "Alright," she whispered, her voice a mixture of trepidation and determination. "I want go with you, Auzrael. To the demon kingdom."

In a tender embrace that seemed to bridge the gap between their worlds, Auzrael held Elvira close. Their bodies pressed together, his touch a mixture of comfort and reassurance as he prepared to transport them to the unfamiliar realm of the demon kingdom. Elvira's heart raced with a blend of anticipation and apprehension, her fingers gripping the fabric of his attire as if holding onto an anchor in the midst of a storm.

Auzrael's eyes met hers, his gaze a reflection of understanding and support. And then, with a surge of power that seemed to ripple through the very fabric of reality, they vanished from the glade, transported through space and time to a place entirely different.

Elvira and Auzrael stay in the forests for a while until Elvira recovers from the fresh wound. And then they return to the demon kingdom.

When they materialized, Elvira found herself in a room unlike any she had ever seen. The atmosphere was different—charged with a unique energy that resonated with the essence of the demon realm. The architecture was intricate and ornate, yet it carried an air of elegance and refinement that surprised her.

Auzrael's grip on her remained steady as he released her from their embrace, his eyes holding a mixture of concern and anticipation. "Welcome to my realm, Elvira," he said softly, his voice a comforting presence amidst the unfamiliar surroundings.

Elvira's gaze swept across the room, Auzrael's room within the demon kingdom exuded an air of grandeur and refinement fit for a ruler, a blend of opulence and elegance that showcased his status. As Elvira stepped into the chamber, her senses were immediately captivated by the intricate details that adorned every corner. The room seemed to be a manifestation of the demon realm's essence, a testament to its otherworldly beauty.

The walls were adorned with dark, rich tapestries that depicted scenes from the demon kingdom's history—majestic battles, ancient rituals, and mesmerizing landscapes. The fabrics seemed to shimmer with an ethereal glow, casting a play of shadows that danced across the room, adding to the mystique.

The flooring was a mosaic of polished stone, adorned with patterns that seemed to tell a story of their own. Runes and symbols were expertly etched into the surface, their meanings known only to those who could decipher them. Soft, velvety rugs were strategically placed in areas of frequent use, providing a plush contrast to the coolness of the stone.

Furniture of dark, polished wood and intricate metalwork adorned the space. A grand four-poster bed dominated one corner, its canopy draped with sumptuous fabrics that cascaded down like a waterfall of midnight hues. Elaborate carvings adorned the bed's headboard, depicting scenes of myth and legend. The bedding was luxurious, a symphony of rich fabrics that invited rest and comfort.

A sitting area was arranged near a large window, the panes of glass offering a breathtaking view of the demon kingdom beyond. Plush cushions and velvet chairs were strategically placed around a low table, creating an inviting space for conversation and contemplation. The room seemed to strike a balance between regality and intimacy, offering both solitude and an environment fit for social gatherings.

Artifacts and trinkets adorned various surfaces, each holding a significance that added to the room's unique charm. Crystal vases held otherworldly flowers that seemed to glow with an inner light, while ornate candelabras offered a warm and flickering glow. Shelves were lined with ancient tomes and scrolls, a testament to Auzrael's knowledge and his connection to the realm's history.

"It's... different," she admitted, her voice a hushed whisper as she tried to process the new reality before her.

Auzrael offered a reassuring smile, his presence a steady anchor amidst the sea of change. "Yes, it is," he agreed. "But I promise you, you will not be alone here. There are humans who have found their place, their purpose, within these walls."

He gestured around the room, his eyes reflecting a genuine sincerity. "This is where you'll stay, Elvira. My room. A sanctuary amidst the demon kingdom."

Elvira's eyes met his, gratitude and vulnerability intertwined in her gaze. "Thank you, Auzrael. For everything."

Auzrael's gaze held hers, his expression a mixture of fondness and a certain gravitas that indicated the weight of his next words. "Elvira," he began gently, "we cannot be the same here as we were outside these walls. In the demon kingdom, our connection must remain hidden from prying eyes."

Elvira's brows furrowed slightly, a flicker of confusion dancing in her eyes. "But why? If we're together, why should we hide it?"

Auzrael's fingers brushed against her cheek, his touch tender as he explained, "The dynamics of this realm are complex, Elvira.

Relationships between humans and demons are... unconventional, to say the least. It could invite scrutiny, danger even."

Her heart sank at the realization, the weight of their reality pressing upon her. Auzrael continued, his voice laced with a mixture of regret and necessity, "For your safety, for both of our safety, it's essential that our connection remains a secret."

Elvira's gaze dropped, a swirl of emotions churning within her. She understood the need for caution, for protecting the delicate balance they were striving to maintain. But the thought of having to conceal the depth of their bond felt like a bittersweet compromise.

"I know it's not easy," Auzrael's voice held a note of understanding, his thumb caressing her cheek. "But you won't be alone in this. There are humans in the demon kingdom who have built their lives here, who have carved out a place amidst the darkness."

He stepped back slightly, his gaze unwavering as he continued, "You'll have to blend in, work alongside them. It's the best way to remain unnoticed and to ensure your safety."

Elvira's shoulders slumped, a mixture of resignation and uncertainty settling over her. "I... I understand."

Auzrael nodded, his gaze holding a promise of support.

Auzrael materialized within the fae realm, his presence cloaked in an aura of tension and purpose. His eyes gleamed with an intensity that spoke of resolve as he cast a piercing gaze across the familiar landscape. Without hesitation, he extended his hands, conjuring dark flames that danced and flickered to life.

The flames licked at the edges of the ethereal realm, consuming the beauty that once defined it. Auzrael's expression remained unyielding, his actions deliberate and driven by a desire for retribution.

As the fire raged, consuming the lush foliage and vibrant colors, the queen herself appeared before him, her regal presence contrasting with the chaos that unfolded. Her gaze held a mixture of shock and accusation as she approached him.

"Why, Auzrael?" Her voice held a note of disbelief, a question that reverberated through the smoky air. "What purpose does this destruction serve?"

Auzrael's eyes bore into hers, his response laden with a chilling calmness. "An eye for an eye," he stated, his words carrying the weight of his actions. He remembered on how the queen had told Elvira- a life for a life.

The queen's expression twisted in a blend of anger and confusion. "This accomplishes nothing but furthering the cycle of pain and chaos. Is vengeance truly worth the cost?"

Auzrael's features remained impassive, his stance unwavering. "It's a reminder, a reflection of the pain inflicted upon Elvira. A glimpse into the torment she has endured."

The queen's gaze narrowed, her voice tinged with both concern and warning. "And what of Elvira? What role does she play in this?"

Auzrael's eyes momentarily softened, a glimmer of emotion breaking through his stoic façade. "She is a survivor, a soul burdened by tragedy. I will protect her, even if it means exacting a price from those who caused her suffering."

The flames continued to consume the realm, the very fabric of the fae world unraveling in the wake of Auzrael's wrath. The queen's expression shifted, a mixture of resignation and understanding crossing her features.

"Your actions have consequences, Auzrael," she cautioned, her voice heavy with a sense of finality.

Auzrael's gaze met hers, his resolve unshaken. "As do yo."

With those words, he turned away, his form dissolving into the shadows as he left behind a realm in turmoil. The flames roared, a stark symbol of the chaos that now mirrored the torment Elvira had endured. And as the realm burned, a somber truth settled within both the fae and the demon realms—a truth that echoed the age-old adage: an eye for an eye.

Chapter 13

Elvira's POV

The chamber embraced me with its opulent warmth as I lay upon the plush bed, its layers of soft fabric cradling me in comfort. The gentle flicker of flames from the hearth cast a mesmerizing dance of light and shadow upon the walls, creating an otherworldly ambiance that soothed my restless heart.

The room held a scent—a faint but unmistakable trace of him. Auzrael. Earth and fire intermingled, an aroma that whispered of his presence and wrapped around me like a gentle caress. It was a fragrance that both comforted and anchored me, as if he were right there beside me, a silent guardian watching over my dreams.

My breathing fell into a rhythm, a soft cadence that matched the tranquility of the room. As my eyes grew heavy, I felt the tendrils of slumber beckoning, drawing me into their embrace. The whispers of dreams swirled around me, promising a respite from the turmoil that had plagued my waking hours.

In the midst of this delicate dance between consciousness and dreams, a faint rustling reached my ears. My heart skipped a beat, a mixture of anticipation and wonder coursing through me. And then, his form emerged from the shadows—the very embodiment of the night.

Auzrael's presence was a blend of grace and ethereal allure. His eyes, illuminated by the soft glow of the hearth, met mine with a tenderness that resonated deep within me. He approached the bed, his steps as light as a whisper, and a smile tugged at the corners of his lips—an unspoken greeting that held more warmth than any words could convey.

As he leaned down, his lips brushed against my forehead in a delicate kiss. It was a gesture that spoke of solace, a promise of protection woven into the fabric of the night. I felt a flutter in my chest, a surge of emotions that defied description, and I found myself longing to stay within this moment forever.

Auzrael slipped beneath the covers, his presence a comforting warmth that enveloped me. The bed shifted slightly as he settled beside me, his arm drawing me close until my head rested against his chest. My breath caught, his heartbeat echoing in my ear like a whispered secret—a rhythmic lullaby that lulled me deeper into the realm of dreams.

I stirred, a contented sigh escaping my lips as if my subconscious recognized the nearness of the one who had become my protector and confidant. His embrace felt both familiar and new, a paradoxical sensation that anchored me to the present and yet hinted at a future unknown.

In this intimate embrace, amidst the quiet of the night, we lay intertwined. The dance of flames continued, casting their gentle glow upon us, creating a cocoon of serenity that held back the weight of the world. As slumber tugged at the edges of my consciousness, I held onto this moment—a moment of solace, of companion-ship, and the unspoken promise that in this realm of shadows and dreams, I was not alone. Auzrael, was by my side, watching over me as I surrendered to the embrace of sleep.

The morning sun cast a pale, diffused light across the demon kingdom as I stepped into the bustling courtyard. A sense of trep-idation clung to me, mingling with the strange mixture of anticipa-tion and anxiety that had become my constant companions since arriving here. I was no longer the Elvira who had stumbled upon Auzrael in the forest, lost and alone, but rather a newcomer to this world that held both beauty and darkness.

Around me, other humans bustled with the energy of purpose, a collective determination etched across their faces. They were like me, outsiders thrust into this realm for reasons unknown, faces marked by a shared uncertainty. Some were tending to gardens that held unearthly flora, while others were engaged in tasks that seemed both ordinary and surreal within the context of the demon kingdom.

Amidst the controlled chaos, my eyes fell upon a figure that sent a shiver down my spine—Behomath. The very demon who had orchestrated the allocation of tasks for the new recruits. He stood tall and imposing, a commanding presence that radiated authority. His eyes seemed to flicker with a glint of amusement as they landed upon me, and I felt a pang of unease.

As I approached, Behomath's lips curled into a knowing smile, an expression that held a hint of mystery. He held a scroll in one hand, its contents undoubtedly detailing the assignments for each of us. My heart raced as I stood before him, unable to shake the feeling that something significant was about to unfold.

"Elvira," his voice rumbled, carrying an air of formality. "I have a special task for you."

A mixture of curiosity and anxiety tightened within me. I waited, my gaze fixed upon him, as he unrolled the scroll and scanned its contents. A silence hung in the air, pregnant with anticipation, until his gaze lifted to meet mine once more.

"You shall be the personal maid to Auzrael, the Prince of Shadows," he declared, his voice carrying the weight of revelation.

Time seemed to stand still as his words settled over me. Auzrael's true identity—the fact that he was not just a mere demon but held a title of power and nobility—was unveiled in an instant. My mind raced, processing the implications of this revelation.

Auzrael was a prince. Auzrael was royalty within this realm that had once seemed so foreign and distant. The pieces of the puzzle fell into place, connecting the enigmatic dots that had eluded me. It explained his presence, his demeanor, his ability to wield both darkness and compassion.

Behomath's gaze bore into mine, as if he could read the maelstrom of thoughts that swirled within me. "Auzrael has chosen you for this role, Elvira. It is a position of honor, but also one of discretion. You will be expected to serve him faithfully and maintain his privacy. Your first task is to prepare the prince for the royal breakfast."

My heart raced, torn between the weight of the revelation and the surge of emotion that threatened to overwhelm me. Auzrael, the Prince of Shadows. My protector, my confidant, held a position of authority that transcended the boundaries of the demon kingdom.

"As his maid," Behomath continued, his tone carrying a note of warning, "you will tread carefully. Your interactions will remain concealed, known only to those who hold positions of trust."

I nodded, my mind a whirlwind of emotions. The gravity of my new role settled upon me—the privilege of being by Auzrael's side, yet the responsibility of preserving the secrecy that shrouded our connection.

Behemoth's smile held a mixture of cryptic wisdom as he handed me a small, ornate key. "This key unlocks the door to his private chamber. It is a symbol of trust and an acknowledgement of the bond that exists between you."

As the key touched my palm, a rush of emotions coursed through me. Gratitude, determination, and an unwavering resolve to fulfill my newfound role to the best of my ability.

I watched as Behomath turned away, his presence a looming figure that faded into the backdrop of the bustling courtyard. Auzrael, the Prince of Shadows, was no longer just a mystery cloaked in darkness. He was a figure of significance, a leader in this realm that I had come to inhabit.

With the weight of the key in my hand and the knowledge of my task, I took a deep breath. My journey had taken an unexpected turn, guiding me deeper into a world of demons and secrets. As I walked towards the door that led to Auzrael's private chamber, I couldn't help but wonder what lay ahead—what challenges, revelations, and choices awaited me as the personal maid to the enigmatic Prince of Shadows.

The entrance to Auzrael's private chamber swung open with a determined force, its hinges breaking the tranquil hush that had enveloped the room. My heart raced as I stood there, my chest heaving with a blend of urgency and disbelief. Auzrael, lost in dreams until that very moment, was abruptly awakened. His eyes blinked against the intrusion, adjusting to the gentle glow that seeped through the draperies.

And there he was, before me, the soft light casting a muted radiance upon him, as he sat up, a hint of amusement dancing in his eyes. "Ah, Elvira," he uttered, his voice carrying a teasing melody. "It appears you've stumbled upon one of my closely guarded secrets."

My gaze remained fixed on him, a whirlwind of amazement and incredulity swirling within me. "Auzrael!" I exclaimed, my voice a mix of astonishment and shock. "You're... you're the prince?"

A playful smile curved his lips, and I couldn't help but feel a rush of emotions in his presence. "Is it truly such a stretch of imagination?" he responded, a mock offense tainting his tone.

I shook my head, laughter and disbelief bubbling from me. "I mean, all this time, you've been by my side, protecting me, and I never even knew..."

His laughter blended harmoniously with mine, the room itself seemed to take on a brighter aura as our shared amusement danced through the air. "I must confess, keeping this hidden from you has indeed proven to be a most delightful challenge," I admitted.

A newfound mirth twinkled in my eyes as I ventured a step closer to him. "So, what other enigmatic secrets do you hold? Might you possess a concealed sanctuary adorned with treasures beyond imagination?"

Auzrael's laughter resonated, his eyes locking onto mine with an unspoken bond. "Perhaps that shall remain a mystery for another time," he responded, his tone laced with secrecy.

I playfully rolled my eyes, a mischievous grin playing at the corners of my lips. "You undeniably possess a remarkable talent for catching me off guard."

He replied with a wink, "Dearest Elvira, that is but one of my numerous skills."

Auzrael's grin broadened, mirroring the mischief twinkling in my eyes. "Ah, believe me, my surprises for you have only just begun," he murmured, his voice a velvety blend of low tones and playful intent.

Before I could react, his movements unfolded with grace and swiftness. In an instant, the gap between us disappeared, his strong form pressed gently against mine. Laughter transformed into a gasp of astonishment as I found myself effortlessly flipped onto the bed, the plush mattress giving way beneath me. Auzrael's strength and agility shone brilliantly, a testament to the potent might inherent in his demon guise.

I was now beneath him, my back against the plush bedding, with my heart racing as his frame caged me in a tantalizing proximity. Auzrael's eyes locked onto mine, his gaze intense yet filled with a playful spark that danced in their depths. His fingers trailed a feather-light path along my jawline, sending a shiver down my spine.

"Caught you," he whispered, his breath warm against my skin, a hint of triumph in his voice.

My lips curved into a mixture of amusement and anticipation. "You certainly did," I admitted, my voice carrying a teasing undertone.

Auzrael's lips quirked in response, his fingers trailing downward to trace the contours of my collarbone. His touch ignited a trail of sensations, each point of contact sending a jolt of awareness through me.

"You know," he mused, his voice dropping to a husky murmur, "I have a feeling that you enjoy being surprised."

I held my gaze to his, a playful glimmer reflecting his unspoken challenge. "And what if I do? What will you do about it?"

Auzrael's laughter was a soft, melodic sound that resonated within the intimate space. "Well, my dear Elvira, I'm afraid I'll have to ensure that you're thoroughly entertained."

Before I could even react, his lips met mine in a kiss that sent waves of electricity and tenderness through my entire being. In that moment, the world around us faded away, leaving only the two of us and the intricate web of emotions that entwined us. His kiss was a delicate balance between passion and restraint, a testament to the intricate threads that defined our connection.

My fingers found their way into the fabric of his shirt, a subconscious urge to bring him closer as I met his kiss with equal intensity. It was as if the weight of our shared secrets, our moments together, and the silent vows we had made all converged in this instance—a moment that felt like both an ending and a fresh start.

When we finally parted, our breaths mingling in the air, his gaze locked onto mine, a blend of yearning and tenderness in his expression. "Surprises, my dear Elvira, are only the beginning," he murmured.

I couldn't help but smile, a spark of excitement lighting up my eyes. "I can't wait to discover what you have in store," I replied, a sense of anticipation bubbling within me.

"I never would have guessed," I confessed, my voice softening as I continued, "But I suppose it makes sense. You've always had this air of... nobility about you."

Auzrael's smile softened, his eyes holding a warmth that matched the gentle light in the room. "I am a prince, but that is just one facet of who I am. What truly matters to me is the connection we share, Elvira."

My cheeks tinged with a faint blush, and I looked away momentarily, playing with the edge of Auzael's collar. "I appreciate that, Auzrael. It's just... a lot to take in."

He reached out, his fingers gently lifting my chin to meet his gaze. "I understand. And I promise, you don't have to navigate this revelation alone. I'm still the same Auzrael you've come to know, regardless of titles."

I met his gaze, and in that moment, we shared an unspoken understanding—a bond that transcended the secrets and complexities of their respective roles. As we sat together in the quiet intimacy of his chamber, the weight of their connection hung in the air—a connection that had been woven through trials, revelations, and a journey that was far from over.

With a soft smile, Auzrael leaned in, his lips brushing against my forehead in a gesture of comfort and reassurance. "You're here, Elvira, and that's all that truly matters."

My heart fluttered, and I leaned into his touch, a sense of contentment settling over me. In that moment, as our worlds intertwined once more, I couldn't help but feel that perhaps destiny had guided me to this realm—a realm where a prince and a human had found an unexpected and extraordinary connection.

"Alright, your highness," I teased, a mischievous twinkle in my eyes. "As much as I enjoy your princely charm, I think it's time for you to move that noble butt of yours and get cleaned up."

Auzrael's eyes glimmered with amusement, his lips curving into a knowing smile. "My dear Elvira," he replied, his tone dripping with feigned innocence, "I believe it's my princely duty to keep you entertained."

I rolled my eyes playfully, a grin tugging at the corners of my lips. "Oh, I have no doubt about your entertainment skills. But even a prince needs to attend to the basics, you know."

Auzrael chuckled, a low and melodic sound that resonated within the room. "Very well, my lady," he conceded with an exaggerated sigh. "I shall heed your advice and attend to the matter at hand."

As he rose from the bed, I couldn't help but watch him with a mixture of amusement and appreciation. Despite his playful demeanor, there was a grace and allure to his movements that held me captivated.

Auzrael turned to me, his eyes locking onto hers with an intensity that sent a shiver down her spine. "But I must warn you," he continued, his voice a low, velvety whisper, "I may require your assistance."

I arched an eyebrow, my curiosity piqued. "Assistance? And what, pray tell, might that entail?"

Auzrael stepped closer, his proximity sending my heart into a frenzy. "Well," he began, his tone laden with a hint of seduction, "a proper bath requires thorough cleansing, does it not? And I've heard that the company of a charming and resourceful maiden can make the experience all the more enjoyable."

My cheeks flushed, a mixture of surprise and anticipation coursing through me. "Oh, is that so?" I replied, playful challenging him. "And how exactly do you envision this 'assistance'?"

Auzrael's fingers brushed a strand of hair away from my face, his touch sending a jolt of electricity through me. "Well," he murmured, his lips hovering dangerously close to mine, "I suppose we'll have to find out, won't we?"

A mischievous glint danced in my eyes as I leant forward, my lips teasingly brushing against Auzrael's ear. "Oh, I have a feeling, Auzrael," I whispered, "that you might not be quite prepared for the level of assistance I can offer."

Auzrael's breath caught, a spark of surprise and intrigue igniting within his eyes. Elvira's boldness had caught him off guard, and he found himself momentarily at a loss for words.

I pulled back slightly, my lips curving into a playful smile. "After all," I continued, with my tone dripping with playful innocence, "a proper bath is a delicate art, requiring attention to every inch. I wouldn't want you to miss a spot."

Auzrael's composure wavered, a mixture of amusement and flustered surprise evident in his expression. His attempts to maintain his princely demeanor were faltering in the face of Elvira's newfound confidence.

I stepped closer, my fingers tracing a teasing path along the edge of his jawline. "But don't worry," I added with a wink, "I'm here to ensure you're thoroughly taken care of."

Auzrael's lips curved into a mixture of amusement and vulnerability. He had always been the one to take the lead, to guide their interactions, but now, the tables had turned. It was a delightful reversal that both intrigued and delighted him.

"Is that so?" he replied, his voice a soft, almost breathless murmur.

I stared into his eyes, a challenge and a promise in his eyes. "Indeed," I affirmed, my fingers now trailing a tantalizing path down his chest.

Auzrael's resolve wavered further, his self-assured façade crumbling as my touch ignited a fire within him. He cleared his throat, attempting to regain his composure. "Well, my dear Elvira," he managed, his voice tinged with a mixture of playfulness and desire, "it appears that the student has become the teacher."

Elvira's laughter was a melodic sound that resonated within the room, a symphony of shared amusement and connection. "I suppose we're both on a learning journey," I remarked, having my tone a sultry invitation.

Auzrael's gaze held mine, the air between us charged with a newfound tension. "Then, by all means, enlighten me," he replied, his voice dropping to a husky whisper.

With a confidence that belied my earlier uncertainty, I leaned in, my lips brushing against his in a kiss that was both bold and tender. I immediately stopped and prepared his bath smirking to myself.

Oh how the roles had shifted.

Chapter 14

E lvira carefully prepared the bath, ensuring the water was warm and inviting, scented with fragrant oils that filled the air with a soothing aroma. As she meticulously arranged the towels and bath salts.

Once everything was ready, "Your bath is ready, Auzrael," she called out.

Auzrael's voice floated from within. "Ah, perfect timing, Elvira. You truly have a gift for making even the simplest things feel like a royal indulgence."

She smiled at his words and stepped back, allowing him privacy as he entered the bath. "Enjoy, my lord."

As Auzrael stepped into the water, a contented sigh escaped his lips. Elvira's heart skipped a beat as she caught sight of him, bare chest and relaxed in the warm bath. His eyes met hers, a mischievous glint dancing within them. He lifted his thighs just enough for her to become flustered. Inviting her to scrub his skin.

"Isn't it customary for attendants to join their lords in the bath, Elvira?" Auzrael's voice was laced with playful teasing.

Elvira's cheeks turned a delicate shade of pink, and she averted her gaze for a moment, her heart racing at his remark. "I-I'm here to ensure your comfort, my lord, not to intrude."

"I believe your task was to prepare wasn't it, Elvira?" He raised his eyebrow.

Elvira's eyes flickered back to him, a mixture of surprise and amusement in her gaze. "I believe you are a grown-up man and can bath by himself."

He grinned, his expression filled with a charming playfulness. "Do you want to be punished or rewarded like the time where you greedily sucked my-"

Elvira's face turned red, "ok, ok, I'll scrub you, please do not taunt me anymore."

As Auzrael lounged in the bath, Elvira couldn't help but feel a warmth spread through her.

Elvira poured a ladle of warm water over Auzrael's shoulders, the soft trickle of liquid creating a soothing rhythm in the bathing chamber. She couldn't help but admire the relaxed expression on his face as he leaned back against the edge of the tub, his eyes closed in contentment.

"Ah, Elvira, you truly have a talent for turning a simple bath into a luxurious experience," Auzrael remarked with a grin, his voice carrying a hint of playful admiration.

Elvira couldn't suppress a chuckle. "I'm glad you're enjoying it, my lord. It's important to find moments of relaxation amidst your princely duties."

Auzrael's eyes flickered open, his gaze locking onto hers. "And do you not believe in taking a moment for yourself, Elvira? I'm sure attending to me keeps you quite occupied."

She dipped a cloth into the fragrant water, carefully wringing it out before gently wiping his arm. "I find fulfillment in my work, Auzrael."

"Scrub harder, Elvira. Do you want me to stink infront of everyone?"

Elvira's cheeks flushed as Auzrael's playful complaint rang in her ears. She held the scrubbing cloth with a touch more determination, applying a gentle pressure to his back as she worked to cleanse his skin.

"Apologies, my lord," she replied, her tone carrying a mixture of amusement and mock seriousness. "I wouldn't dare let such a fate befall you."

Auzrael let out a dramatic sigh, his lips curling into a grin. "Ah, I knew I could count on you to ensure my olfactory reputation remains untarnished."

As Elvira bent beside the tub she looked at the powerful thighs that she had once grabbed. Heat pooled through her core. She rubbed her thighs and hoped that the cocky demon doesn't smell her arousal that filled her.

"Are you waiting for an invitation to scrub my chest?" Auzrael smirked, looking at his nails though he freshly painted them.

"No, my lord." Elvira brought the scrub to his chest and scrubbed it, his chest was so fine. She quickly composed herself and finished his bath, handing his towel she rushed out of the room.

Elvira stood just outside the chamber, her heart beating a little faster with anticipation. She had meticulously arranged Auzrael's attire, ensuring every detail was in place. Her eyes fluttered to the door as it opened, revealing Auzrael, now dressed in his princely garments.

Her breath caught in her throat as she took in the sight before her. Auzrael's presence seemed to fill the corridor, his posture radiating confidence and regal grace. He moved with a certain elegance, each step imbued with a kingly manner that seemed almost otherworldly.

The rich fabric of his clothing draped perfectly, accentuating his tall and commanding figure. The deep hues of his attire complemented his features, enhancing his already striking presence. His eyes, always filled with a captivating intensity, now held a certain air of authority that sent a shiver down Elvira's spine.

For a fleeting moment, time seemed to stand still as Elvira drank in the sight of him. Auzrael was more than a prince; he was a living embodiment of royalty, every inch of him exuding power and dignity. Her admiration for him deepened, mingling with a newfound awareness of the complexities that lay beneath the surface.

As Auzrael approached, his lips curved into a warm smile, breaking the spell that had momentarily entranced Elvira. "Well, Elvira, do I pass the royal inspection?"

Her cheeks tinged with a delicate blush, and she offered a soft chuckle. "Indeed, my lord. You possess a truly kingly presence."

Auzrael's smile widened, a playful glint in his eyes. "Ah, I see my efforts have met with your approval."

Elvira nodded.

As they began to walk down the corridor. Elvira trailed behind Auzrael.

Elvira stood silently behind the ornate dining table, her posture composed and her expression neutral. The grand hall was abuzz with the voices of the royal family, engaged in a discussion of political matters that held the fate of the kingdom in their hands.

Elvira's focus, however, remained on her duty—to serve Auzrael, to anticipate his needs, and to ensure his comfort.

Auzrael sat at the head of the table, his regal presence commanding the attention of all those present. His voice was steady and authoritative as he contributed to the conversation, discussing matters of diplomacy and strategy with a shrewdness that belied his youthful appearance. The weight of his responsibilities seemed to press upon him, and his demeanor was distant, a stark contrast to the warmth she had witnessed in private moments.

Elvira's heart ached as she observed him from afar, her instincts urging her to approach and attend to him. Yet, she remained patient, waiting for Auzrael's signal, for his subtle gesture that would indicate he required her assistance. Her loyalty to her duty was unwavering, even in the face of his apparent indifference.

Finally, Auzrael's gaze shifted, his eyes meeting hers for a fleeting moment. It was the unspoken cue Elvira had been waiting for. With practiced grace, she approached the table, her steps measured and her expression carefully neutral.

"Your Highness," she murmured softly, addressing Auzrael as she reached his side.

He barely spared her a glance, his attention still fixed on the ongoing conversation. "Elvira, my goblet is empty. See to it."

Elvira's heart clenched at the coldness in his tone, but she maintained her composure. She refilled his goblet with wine, her movements efficient and respectful. She then offered a plate of assorted fruits and pastries, silently awaiting his selection.

Auzrael's hand lazily gestured toward a particular pastry, his voice devoid of warmth. "That one, and bring me black tea."

Elvira placed the pastry onto his plate, her gaze remaining lowered. She could feel the scrutinizing eyes of the royal family upon her, their curiosity and judgment adding to the weight of the moment.

Elvira nodded in response to Auzrael's command, her heart heavy with the weight of his distant demeanor. She silently moved away from the table, her steps graceful yet carrying a sense of resignation. As she walked towards the sideboard to fetch the requested black tea, her thoughts churned, unable to shake off the coldness that had enveloped Auzrael's words.

As Elvira moved to the sideboard to pour the tea, the queen's voice cut through the atmosphere. "Speaking of engagements, it reminds me of the recent union between Prince Auzrael and Princess Isabella. A joyous occasion for both our kingdoms."

Elvira's heart skipped a beat, her movements faltering for a brief moment as the words settled around her like a heavy shroud. She carefully continued pouring the tea, her fingers gripping the delicate teapot a bit too tightly. The mention of Auzrael's engagement, something she had been entirely unaware of until now, shattered the fragile hope that had lingered within her.

Auzrael's reaction was almost imperceptible, a slight tensing of his shoulders as he took a sip of his tea. His gaze remained fixed on his cup, his expression guarded.

Elvira's breath caught in her throat as the reality of the situation washed over her. The man she had come to care for, the one promised to show her kindness and vulnerability, was bound by duty to another. Their private moments, their shared laughter and fleeting touches, now felt like distant memories.

She forced herself to regain her composure, her heartache hidden behind a mask of professionalism. With steady hands, she carried the cup of tea to Auzrael and placed it before him, her gaze fixed on the table as she retreated a step.

"Is there anything else you require, Your Highness?" Elvira's voice was steady, though a subtle quiver betrayed her emotions.

Auzrael's response was curt, his attention still seemingly elsewhere. "No, you may leave."

Elvira gave a slight nod, her chest constricting with a mix of sadness and unspoken words. She retreated from the grand hall, her steps steady even as her world seemed to crumble around her.

The queen's words continued to echo in her mind as she moved through the corridors, her thoughts consumed by the realization of Auzrael's engagement. The hopes she had dared to harbor had been dashed, replaced by the cold reality of their respective stations.

Elvira paused in a quiet alcove, her emotions finally breaking through the façade she had maintained. Silent tears slid down her cheeks as she grappled with the ache in her heart—the ache of unrequited feelings that had taken root despite her best efforts to suppress them.

Her breath shuddered as she leaned against the cool stone wall, her fingers clenching into fists at her sides. She scolded herself inwardly, her thoughts a maelstrom of self-blame and frustration.

"How foolish I am," she whispered to herself, her voice tinged with a mix of anguish and anger. "To have allowed myself to fall for him, to let my heart entwine with his, knowing the boundaries that fate has placed between us."

Elvira returned to Auzrael's chambers, the soft glow of candlelight casting a warm ambiance within the room. She took a deep breath, her resolve solidifying as she retrieved her notebook and a quill from the small desk. Sitting down in a comfortable chair, she began to scribble, pouring her thoughts and emotions onto the pages, allowing the ink to become a vessel for her inner turmoil.

The hours slipped by as Elvira lost herself in the act of writing, her thoughts flowing freely from her heart onto the paper. The scratching of the quill against the parchment became a rhythmic melody, a soothing balm for her wounded soul.

As the night deepened, the door to the chamber creaked open, and Auzrael's figure entered. Elvira's heart skipped a beat, but she maintained her composure, her expression a mask of neutrality. She set the quill aside and rose from her seat, facing him with a respectful distance.

"Your Highness," she addressed him, her tone even and devoid of any hint of sarcasm or emotion.

Auzrael's steps faltered slightly, his brows knitting in confusion as he looked at her. Her distant demeanor was unexpected, and he found himself puzzled by the change in her behavior. They had agreed to keep their relationship private, a decision they had made to protect both of them from potential repercussions.

He cleared his throat, his voice carrying a note of sincerity. "Elvira, is something amiss?"

Elvira met his gaze, her expression still carefully neutral. "No, Your Highness. I am simply fulfilling my duties as your attendant."

Auzrael's confusion deepened, his gaze searching hers for any sign of what might have triggered this shift. He knew they were in a delicate situation, but he hadn't anticipated her to be this distant.

"Elvira," he began, his tone gentle, "I did not mean for our private understanding to result in such coldness between us. Have I unknowingly caused offense?"

She shook her head, her voice measured. "You have done nothing wrong, Your Highness. I am merely maintaining the decorum expected of me."

Auzrael's concern for her wellbeing only grew, and he took a step closer. "Elvira, please, tell me what troubles you. Our agreement was made to protect us both. I never intended for you to feel this way."

Elvira hesitated, her resolve momentarily faltering as she looked into his eyes. She had built these walls to shield herself, but the genuine worry in his voice chipped at the defenses she had constructed.

"Why have you brought me here, Your Highness?" she asked, her voice quiet yet unwavering. "Especially when you are promised to another."

Auzrael's gaze held hers, his eyes sincere and full of emotion. "I brought you here so you can heal, Elvira. So you can mend your heart and find some measure of happiness. You deserve that."

Elvira's lips parted slightly, her heart conflicted as his words resonated within her. She wanted to believe him, to find solace in the idea that he cared for her well-being. Yet, the reality of the situation, the knowledge that he would eventually play the role of a husband with another woman, stirred a whirlwind of emotions within her.

"You speak of healing and happiness, Az," Elvira's voice trembled with anger and pain, her control slipping as her emotions surged forth. "But how can you expect me to find such solace when the very presence of your betrothal, of your impending union with another, is what tears my heart apart?"

Auzrael's expression flickered, a mixture of empathy and regret. "Elvira, I—"

"No," she interrupted, her words laced with frustration. "Do not tell me that this is for the best, that it is for the kingdom's stability. I understand duty, Az, but I will not be a pawn to mend my own heart while watching you play husband to another."

The tension in the room was palpable as Elvira's words hung in the air, her anger and pain laid bare. She took a deep breath, her chest rising and falling as she struggled to regain her composure.

"Return me elsewhere," she said, her voice steadier now, though still infused with a quiet anger. "Return me to the fae, where they can keep me in their dungeons if need be. I will not remain here, a silent witness to a loveless union that I am expected to accept."

Auzrael's expression reflected a mix of turmoil and understanding. He reached out, his hand hovering in the space between them, a silent plea for her to listen. "Elvira, I never intended for you to be hurt in this way. I did not foresee the depth of your pain."

Elvira's gaze met his, her anger tempered by the sincerity she saw in his eyes. "Auzrael, I do not doubt your intentions. But you must understand the conflict within me. To be by your side, to witness you with another, it is a torment I cannot endure."

Auzrael lowered his hand, his shoulders slumping as he absorbed her words. "Elvira, I care for you deeply-"

Elvira's anger began to ebb, replaced by a lingering sadness that weighed heavily upon her. "Az, I appreciate your concern, but I must prioritize my own well-being. I cannot stay here, caught between my feelings for you and the reality of our circumstances."

Auzrael nodded slowly, his expression a mixture of regret and acceptance. "If you believe it is best, Elvira, I will honor your wishes. But know that my concern for you remains genuine."

Elvira's heart raced as she looked at him, her emotions at once a tumultuous sea. The sight of him stirred a wellspring of feelings she had been grappling with, and before she could fully comprehend her own actions, her hand shot out, her palm connecting with his chest in a sharp, unexpected motion.

"You fool!" she exclaimed, her voice carrying a blend of anger and hurt. "You speak of concern for my well-being, yet you agree to send me away when I confessed my feelings for you?"

Auzrael staggered back slightly, his eyes wide with surprise. His hand instinctively moved to where she had struck him, his confusion evident in his features.

"Elvira, I... I did not anticipate your confession," he stammered, his words laced with bewilderment. "I thought you needed space, time to heal."

Elvira's chest heaved with a mix of emotions, her anger giving way to a torrent of frustration. "And you thought sending me away, like some fragile creature, was the solution?"

Auzrael's brows furrowed, his attempts to understand the situation evident on his face. "Elvira, I do care for you, but I thought—"

"You thought what, Auzrael?" Elvira's voice trembled with a blend of hurt and indignation. "That my feelings could be easily brushed aside? That I would simply accept being cast aside for the sake of appearances?"

Auzrael's expression shifted from confusion to a deepening realization, his gaze locking onto hers as he seemed to grasp the depth of her emotions.

"Elvira, I never meant for you to feel that way," he said, his voice earnest. "I thought I was doing what was best for you."

Elvira's anger began to ebb, replaced by a heavy sense of weariness. She met his gaze, her eyes reflecting the complex mixture of her emotions. "Auzrael, do you not understand? The pain I feel is not just about being away from you. It's about the knowledge that you would choose duty over what we shared."

Auzrael's shoulders sagged, his expression a portrait of regret. "Elvira, I... I did not fully consider the weight of my decision."

Elvira's voice softened, her frustration giving way to a poignant sadness. "Auzrael, I do not resent you for your duties, but I cannot ignore my own heart either. I confessed my feelings because I wanted you to understand, to know the truth. And you agreed to send me away without a second thought."

As Elvira spoke, Auzrael's heart wrenched with the weight of her words. He had never intended to hurt her, and the realization that his actions had caused her pain gnawed at him. He reached out and gently cupped her cheek, his thumb caressing her soft skin.

"Elvira, I never wanted to hurt you," he murmured, his voice filled with remorse. "I care for you deeply, and the thought of sending you away pained me too. But I thought it was what you needed."

Elvira's eyes softened, her anger and hurt giving way to a flicker of understanding. She leaned into his touch, seeking solace in the warmth of his hand on her skin. Auzrael's touch was a balm to her wounded heart, and she found herself drawn closer to him, her head resting against his chest. Auzrael's arms encircled her, holding her close as if to shield her from the world.

She tilted her head to meet his gaze, her eyes searching his for any hint of deception. "You do?"

Auzrael nodded, his eyes unwavering as he held her gaze. "Yes, Elvira. The thought of sending you away hurt me too, more than I can express. I want you to be happy, and the idea of being the source of your pain is unbearable."

Elvira's heart swelled with a mixture of emotions, a potent blend of hope and fear intertwining within her. She allowed herself to lean into his embrace, finding solace in his closeness and the unspoken understanding between them.

And then, as if unable to resist his natural inclination for levity, Auzrael's lips curved into a small smile. "Although," he began, his voice teasing, "if I had known that confessing my feelings would lead to such a passionate display of frustration, I might have considered it sooner."

Elvira's eyes widened as his comment disrupted the moment, a surprised laugh escaping her lips. She pulled away slightly, playfully swatting his arm. "You fool," she said, her tone laced with amusement.

Without a word, their lips met in a searing kiss, a collision of longing and desire that ignited a fire within them both. It was a kiss born from the depths of their hearts, a culmination of the unspoken feelings that had simmered beneath the surface for so long.

Auzrael's arms tightened around Elvira, pulling her closer as their lips moved together in a dance that spoke of passion and yearning. The touch of their mouths was electric, a cascade of sensations that sent a rush of warmth through their veins.

Elvira's fingers tangled in Auzrael's hair, her touch gentle yet urgent, as if trying to bridge the gap between them even further. His response was equally fervent, his hands tracing a path along her back, drawing her impossibly nearer.

Time seemed to stand still as they explored the depths of each other's emotions through that kiss, a language that needed no words. It was a kiss that held the promise of a shared future, a testament to their willingness to defy the odds and embrace their feelings against all odds.

Eventually, their lips parted, but the connection between them remained, a fragile thread that bound their hearts together. Auzrael rested his forehead against Elvira's, their breaths mingling in the intimate space they had created.

Chapter 15

A s I went about my tasks in the demon kingdom, my heart skipped a beat when I noticed another demon approaching me. His graceful gait and piercing gaze immediately put me on edge. He didn't wear the royal attire, but there was something about him that hinted at authority.

He stopped in front of me, his eyes narrowing as he studied me. "And who might you be?" he asked, his voice carrying a hint of suspicion.

I tried to maintain a calm facade, but my heart was racing. "I'm just a new servant here," I replied, my voice steady but my nerves on edge.

The demon raised an eyebrow, his gaze lingering on me for a moment longer than I felt comfortable. "A servant, you say?" he questioned, his tone laced with doubt.

"Yes, that's right," I answered, trying my best to appear nonchalant.

He seemed unconvinced, taking a step closer as he scrutinized me further. My mind raced, trying to come up with an explanation that wouldn't blow my cover. I couldn't afford to reveal my true identity as a human in the demon kingdom.

Just as I was beginning to feel trapped, a familiar figure appeared beside me. It was the head servant, a woman who had been kind to me since my arrival. She looked at the other demon with a calm expression, her aura radiating authority.

"Is there a problem here? Your highness." she inquired, her voice cool and collected.

"I was just curious about this new servant," he replied.

The head servant cast a knowing glance at me before turning her attention back to the "highness". "Elvira is new here, but she is under my watch. You need not worry about her."

The prince's gaze remained fixed on me, an intensity that sent a shiver down my spine. "Very well," he repeated, his voice holding a note of finality. "I believe this new servant shall serve in my chambers from now."

My heart sank at his words, realizing that I was now under the direct attention of a member of the royal family whom I have no clue about. I exchanged a quick glance with the head servant, who seemed equally concerned.

"Your Highness, I understand your request, but tasks and assignments are typically handled by Behomath," the head servant spoke up, her tone respectful but firm. "He is in charge of organizing the duties of the servants."

The prince's lips curled into a faint smile, a glimmer of amusement dancing in his eyes. "Ah, Behomath," he mused, his voice carrying a tinge of condescension. "I assure you, I have the authority to make such decisions."

The head servant's expression tightened, a hint of concern crossing her features. "Of course, Your Highness," she replied, her voice carefully neutral. "But it is his role to oversee these matters. I will make sure to discuss this with him- and Elvira is currently assigned to Prince Auzrael."

I held my breath, hoping that her words would be enough to dissuade the prince from his decision.

But the head servant's words seemed to strike a nerve, and a flicker of annoyance crossed the prince's features. His brows furrowed, and his tone took on an edge of impatience. "Are you questioning my authority, Head Servant?" he retorted, his voice laced with a sharpness that cut through the air.

The head servant's gaze held steady, her expression a mix of deference and resolve. "No, Your Highness, not at all," she replied, her voice unwavering. "I merely wish to ensure that proper protocols are followed and that tasks are assigned according to the established procedures."

The prince's lips curled into a cold smile, his eyes narrowing as he regarded her. "It seems you forget your place, Head Servant," he replied, his voice dripping with a biting condescension. "You would do well to remember that your authority is limited to the organization of menial tasks. Matters involving servants of higher rank fall under my purview."

The head servant's posture remained respectful, but there was a subtle tension in her stance. "Of course, Your Highness. I apologize for any misunderstanding."

The prince's gaze remained fixed on her, his frustration evident in the tightness of his jaw. "See that you do not allow such misunderstandings to occur in the future," he warned, his tone cutting. "Now, if you are done questioning my decisions, I have other matters to attend to."

With a curt nod, the head servant stepped back, a hint of deference in her demeanor. "Of course, Your Highness. Your commands will be followed."

As the prince turned and strode away, the air seemed to hang heavy with tension. I watched the exchange from a distance, my heart pounding in my chest. It was clear that the head servant had tried to assert her authority in an effort to protect me, but the prince's response had been swift and harsh.

As the prince turned and walked away, a sense of unease settled over me. The head servant placed a reassuring hand on my shoulder, her expression apologetic. "I tried to prevent this," she whispered.

I nodded, my mind racing with thoughts of how I could navigate this new challenge. "Thank you for trying," I murmured, my voice tinged with both gratitude and worry.

she cautioned, her eyes holding a mixture of concern and determination. "I will speak to Behomath, but until then, do your best to fulfill your duties without drawing unnecessary attention."

With those words, she left me to process the situation on my own. I returned to my tasks, my thoughts consumed by the implications of serving in the prince's chambers. It was a precarious position to be in, and I knew that I would have to tread carefully to avoid any unwanted revelations.

The atmosphere in the grand hall was tense as the royal lunch commenced. I stood at an arm's length from Az, my gaze carefully neutral as I went about my duties. The murmurs of the courtiers and nobles filled the air, creating a backdrop of hushed conversations and stifled tension.

As the meal progressed, a palpable sense of anticipation hung in the air. The presence of the prince who had requested my service was a weighty reminder of the challenges I now faced. My heart raced as I anticipated his next move, knowing that his intentions toward me were far from benign.

The silence was broken by the prince's voice, a taunting edge underlying his words. "Ah, Prince Auzrael," he began, his tone dripping with false camaraderie, "I see you have acquired a new servant. How fortunate for you."

Az's expression remained composed, his gaze steady as he regarded the prince. "Indeed," he replied evenly, his voice carrying a hint of amusement. "Elvira is a valued addition to our household."

The prince's lips curled into a sly smile, his eyes glinting with mischief. "Valued, you say? I'm sure she will prove to be quite... useful in various capacities."

My cheeks warmed, but I kept my focus on my task, maintaining a facade of detachment. The prince's words were a thinly veiled provocation, a calculated attempt to rile Az and assert his dominance.

Az's gaze remained unwavering, his tone cool as he replied, "I have no doubt that Elvira will carry out her duties with the same dedication she has displayed since her arrival."

The prince's laughter was a grating sound that filled the space between them. "Dedication, yes. And I hear you have plans for her beyond these walls. A new servant for the royal chambers, I hear?"

Az's jaw tightened imperceptibly, his control slipping for a brief moment before he regained his composure. "My personal matters are of no concern to you, Your prince Kael."

The prince's gaze bore into Az, a challenge implicit in his stare. "Ah, but they become my concern when they involve a servant under my jurisdiction. After all, it won't be long before we welcome a new addition to the royal family. A soon-to-be wife deserves her own retinue of servants, don't you agree?"

The implications of his words hung in the air, a heavy weight that threatened to shatter the fragile equilibrium. I felt a rush of indignation, but I knew better than to show any sign of weakness. My hands trembled slightly, hidden beneath the folds of my attire, as I continued to serve the dishes.

Az's expression remained inscrutable, his voice a low and controlled murmur. "Your concern is duly noted, Prince Kael. However, my personal affairs remain just that—personal."

The tension in the room seemed to thicken, the air heavy with unspoken words and conflicting emotions. Kael's gaze remained fixed on Az, his own expression a mix of determination and concern.

The queen's gaze shifted to Az, her scrutiny intense. "Is this true, Azrael? Have you formed an attachment to a servant?"

Az met his mother's gaze, his eyes steady. "Mother, my personal matters are not up for public discussion. Rest assured, I am capable of handling my affairs."

"Azrael, you are my son, and your actions reflect not only upon you but upon our entire realm. It is important that you uphold the values and traditions of our people."

Az's expression remained inscrutable, his eyes narrowing slightly as he regarded his mother. The tension in the room seemed to thicken, a silent battle of wills between mother and son. He understood the weight of his mother's words and the expectations that came with his position, but he was unwilling to back down without a fight.

"Mother," he began, his voice firm yet respectful, "I appreciate your concern for the reputation of our family. However, I must make it clear that Elvira is under my care, and I will not dismiss her without just cause."

Queen Seraphina, regal and poised, met her son's gaze with a mix of disappointment and frustration. "Auzrael, you are the prince, the future leader of our realm," she admonished. "Your actions reflect not only upon you but upon the entire demon court. This... attachment you have developed is unbecoming."

Az's jaw clenched, a ripple of conflicting emotions crossing his features. "With all due respect, Mother," he retorted, his tone edged with a hint of defiance, "I have always upheld my responsibilities to the court and our people. My personal choices should not be subject to scrutiny."

she said, her voice gentle yet firm. "But you must consider the consequences of your actions. The demon court is not known for its tolerance of such... relationships."

Az's shoulders stiffened, his resolve unwavering. "Mother, I am well aware of the court's traditions and expectations," he replied. "But I refuse to cast aside someone who has shown unwavering loyalty and dedication."

The queen regarded her son for a long moment, a mix of emotions playing across her features. "Very well," she conceded, her voice carrying a weight of resignation. "If you are determined to keep this servant, then so be it. But remember, Auzrael, your choices have far-reaching consequences."

As the tension in the room seemed to ease slightly, Prince Kael stepped forward, his gaze steady as he addressed the queen. "Your wisdom is invaluable, Mother," he said, his tone respectful. "Perhaps it would be best if we focus on the upcoming diplomatic negotiations. The matters of the heart can wait."

As I scrubbed the floors of Prince Kael's chambers, my mind was a whirlwind of emotions. The recent lunch with the royal family had left me feeling a mixture of frustration and indignation. The way Kael had spoken, the thinly veiled jabs and condescension, had ignited a fire of resentment within me.

I scrubbed harder, my movements fueled by the simmering anger that bubbled just beneath the surface. How dare he treat me as though I were beneath him? As though I were nothing more than a mere servant, unworthy of respect or consideration?

The soapy water sloshed around the bucket as I vigorously cleaned, my thoughts a storm of curses directed at the prince. Who did he think he was, ordering me around and then pretending to be the epitome of politeness in front of his mother? It was infuriating, the way he played his games, manipulating the situation to his advantage.

I scoured the floor with a vengeance, my fingers gripping the scrub brush as if it were Kael's neck. Each swipe was a release of my frustration, a silent declaration that I would not be cowed by his arrogance.

But even as I cursed him in my mind, a nagging voice reminded me of the precarious position I was in. I was a servant in the demon kingdom, and no matter how justified my anger felt, I had to tread carefully. My actions had consequences, not just for me but for Az as well.

As I continued to clean, my thoughts shifted to Az. He had stood up for me, defied his mother's wishes, and put his own reputation on the line. The memory of his unwavering support tempered my anger, reminding me that not all demons were like Kael.

I paused for a moment, taking a deep breath and allowing the anger to dissipate. The cool water and the rhythmic motion of scrubbing had a calming effect, and I knew I couldn't let Kael's behavior consume me.

With renewed determination, I focused on the task at hand, scrubbing away the dirt and frustration. As the floors began to gleam, I felt a small sense of satisfaction. I might not be able to change the prince's attitude, but I could take pride in my own work and resilience.

With a final wipe of the cloth, I stood back to admire the sparkling floors of Prince Kael's chambers. The satisfaction of a job well done was a small victory in the midst of my tumultuous thoughts. I took a moment to catch my breath, a sense of accomplishment washing over me. No matter the challenges I faced, I could always find solace in my own hard work and determination.

However, my brief moment of triumph was shattered when the door to the chamber swung open, revealing Prince Kael. He entered the room with an air of careless nonchalance, his fighting leathers covered in mud and his boots leaving dirty tracks on the pristine floor I had just cleaned. My heart sank, a gasp escaping my lips before I could stop it.

Kael's gaze shifted to me, his expression a mix of surprise and amusement. He seemed completely unfazed by the mess he was creating, his lips curling into a smug smile. "Ah, Elvira," he drawled, his tone dripping with arrogance. "I see you've been hard at work."

I bit my lip, struggling to maintain my composure in the face of his blatant disregard for my efforts. "Yes, Your Highness," I replied, my voice strained but respectful. "I've just finished cleaning the floors."

Kael's eyes flicked down to his mud-caked boots, then back up to meet mine. His smirk widened, as if he took pleasure in the frustration that was undoubtedly written all over my face. "My apologies," he said, his tone laced with false sincerity. "I didn't realize I'd be tracking in so much... dirt."

I clenched my fists at my sides, my frustration threatening to boil over. It was as if he was intentionally trying to provoke a reaction from me. I took a deep breath, reminding myself to stay composed. "I can clean it up again," I offered, my tone controlled but tinged with a hint of irritation.

Kael's smirk only seemed to widen at my response, as if my irritation was some sort of victory for him. He leaned casually against the doorframe, his arms crossed over his chest. "Oh, I have no doubt that you can clean it up again," he said, his voice dripping with condescension. "In fact, I insist that you do. I'd hate to think that my chambers aren't spotless."

I bit back a retort, the urge to snap at him almost overwhelming. Instead, I nodded curtly, my jaw clenched in an effort to keep my emotions in check. "Very well, Your Highness," I replied, my words laced with forced politeness. "I'll make sure it's spotless."

His smirk remained firmly in place as he pushed himself off the doorframe and walked towards me. "Excellent," he purred, his tone like honeyed poison. "And while you're at it, fetch me a cup of coffee. Make it just the way I like it."

The audacity of his request was enough to make my blood boil, but I refused to let him see how much he was getting under my skin. I swallowed my pride and met his gaze with a level stare. "Of course, Your Highness," I replied, my voice steady despite the seething frustration beneath the surface. "I'll have your coffee ready shortly."

He nodded, that infuriating smirk never leaving his lips. "See that you do," he said dismissively, as if he were ordering a servant around rather than speaking to another person.

As he turned to leave, I couldn't help but clench my teeth, a surge of anger coursing through me. It was clear that Kael was enjoying every moment of this power play, reveling in the control he held over me. But I was determined not to let him break me, not to let his arrogance and entitlement dictate my actions.

Once he was gone, I took a deep breath and released the tension that had been building within me. I reminded myself that this was just another challenge, another test of my resilience. With renewed determination, I set to work, cleaning the muddy tracks from the floor with meticulous care.

As I worked, my thoughts turned to the task of making Kael's coffee. I knew that every action I took would be scrutinized, every detail judged. But I was determined to rise above his expectations, to show him that I was more than just a servant fulfilling his whims.

With the floors cleaned to a level of perfection that even Kael couldn't find fault with, I made my way to the kitchen to prepare his coffee. My hands moved with a purpose, measuring out the coffee grounds and water, ensuring that every step was executed flawlessly.

As the rich aroma of freshly brewed coffee filled the air, I poured the steaming liquid into a delicate cup, just the way Kael liked it. I held the cup carefully, my fingers steady despite the nervous anticipation that fluttered in my chest.

Returning to Prince Kael's chambers, I presented the cup of coffee to him with a respectful nod. "Your coffee, Your Highness," I said evenly, my gaze meeting his with unwavering determination. His eyes bore into mine, a silent challenge passing between us as I held the delicate cup in my outstretched hand.

Kael reached out to take the cup from me, his fingers brushing against mine in a deliberate, almost taunting manner. As his hand closed around the cup, a sudden jerk seemed to take him by surprise. The cup slipped from his grasp, hot coffee splashing out and onto my hands.

I couldn't help the sharp gasp that escaped me as the scalding liquid made contact with my skin. Instinctively, I pulled my hands back, my fingers stinging from the heat. The cup fell to the floor, the remaining contents spilling across the polished surface.

Kael's expression remained impassive, as if the spill had been a mere accident. His eyes, however, glinted with something akin to amusement. "Ah, my apologies," he said with a hint of mock concern. "It seems my grip failed me for a moment."

The sting in my hands intensified, a mix of pain and frustration welling up within me. I bit my lip, struggling to maintain my composure despite the discomfort. My gaze met his, a mixture of anger and restraint flashing in my eyes.

Kael's lips curved into a sly smile, his tone dripping with condescension. "Hot coffee has a way of getting away from you, doesn't it? I despise it when it's too hot," he continued, his words laced with a deliberate edge. "Perhaps now you've learned your lesson, Elvira. A valuable skill for a servant, wouldn't you agree?"

My jaw clenched, his thinly veiled mockery fueling my frustration. I fought to keep my voice steady, to prevent the anger from seeping through. "Of course, Your Highness," I replied, my tone a mask of forced deference. "I'll be sure to remember that."

Kael chuckled to himself, the sound a grating reminder of his power over me. "Good," he said, his gaze lingering on my hands, which I had instinctively cradled against my chest. "Accidents can happen, after all. It's important to be cautious, especially when serving someone of my stature."

His words were a deliberate provocation, a reminder of the vast divide between us. I took a deep breath, reminding myself to stay composed, to not give him the satisfaction of seeing my frustration. "I'll clean this up immediately," I said, my voice steady despite the pain throbbing in my hands.

Kael's gaze followed me as I retrieved a cloth and began to wipe up the spilled coffee. His amusement seemed to grow, a twisted satisfaction in seeing me brought low. "Do take your time, Elvira," he remarked, his tone dripping with false politeness. "After all, I wouldn't want you to burn yourself again."

I gritted my teeth, his taunts and condescension testing the limits of my restraint. But I refused to let him break me, to let his arrogance and cruelty define my worth. With each swipe of the cloth, I reminded myself that I was stronger than his words, more resilient than his attempts to undermine me.

Once the spill had been cleaned and the cup discarded, I straightened up and met Kael's gaze head-on. "Is there anything else, Your Highness?" I asked, my voice cool and controlled.

Kael's smirk remained firmly in place, a smug satisfaction radiating from him. "Not at the moment, Elvira," he replied, his tone a mixture of dismissal and amusement. "You may go."

I inclined my head in a respectful nod, my resolve unshaken despite the encounter. Turning on my heel, I left his chambers, the memory of his mocking laughter and the sting of hot coffee on my hands serving as a reminder of the challenges I faced.

As I walked away, I couldn't help but clench my hands into fists, the pain in my palms a tangible reminder of the power dynamics at play. But I was determined to rise above his cruelty, to prove that I was more than just a servant to be ridiculed. With each step, I carried with me a renewed determination to show Kael—and myself—that I was capable of weathering even the harshest storms.

Chapter 16

I sank onto the plush sofa in Az's chamber, my hand cradled protectively against my chest. The searing pain radiating from my burnt palm was a constant reminder of the encounter with Prince Kael. Gritting my teeth, I blew a soft stream of air over the angry red skin, a feeble attempt to soothe the fiery agony that seemed to engulf my entire hand.

The blisters that had formed were an angry shade of red, raised and swollen against my tender flesh. Each touch, each movement, sent a sharp jolt of pain through me, making me wince with every twitch of my fingers. I clenched my teeth together, fighting back tears of frustration and pain.

I studied the blisters, my gaze tracing the contours of the wounds as if willing them to heal faster. The skin was tight and stretched, a stark contrast to the smoothness of my uninjured hand. A thin sheen of sweat formed on my forehead as I continued to blow cool air onto the burn, the slight relief it brought offering a brief respite from the torment.

My other hand trembled slightly as I reached for a nearby cloth. Gently, I wrapped the soft fabric around my burnt palm, creating a makeshift bandage to shield it from further irritation. The touch of the cloth against the blisters was both comforting and painful, a reminder of the delicate balance between seeking relief and avoiding more harm.

Closing my eyes, I took a slow, steadying breath, trying to quell the throbbing ache that pulsed through my hand. The pain seemed to echo with every beat of my heart, a constant reminder of the challenges I faced in this unfamiliar world.

As I sat there, nursing my wounded hand, a mix of emotions swirled within me. Frustration at Kael's callousness, anger at the power dynamics that allowed him to treat me so recklessly, and a simmering determination to prove that I was more than just a servant subjected to his whims.

But beneath it all, there was a quiet resolve—a stubborn refusal to let this setback define me. I was stronger than the pain, stronger than the challenges that lay before me. With each passing moment, as the pain gradually subsided to a dull throb, I found a renewed determination to rise above the trials and carve my own path in this complex and unforgiving realm.

And as I sat on that sofa, cradling my wounded hand and nursing my wounded pride, I knew that I would continue to fight, to endure, and to prove my worth in the face of adversity.

And so, I waited. The passage of time seemed to stretch endlessly as I sat in Az's chamber, my eyes fixed on the intricately carved doorway, hoping for his return. The soft flicker of candlelight cast dancing shadows across the room, a gentle reminder of the world beyond these walls.

My thoughts wandered, a cascade of emotions swirling within me. The pain in my hand had subsided to a dull ache, but my wounded pride still stung. Kael's dismissive attitude and calculated provocations echoed in my mind, a constant undercurrent to my growing determination.

As minutes turned into an hour, the silence in the chamber became more pronounced. It was unlike Az to be absent for this long, especially when he knew I awaited his return. A sliver of unease crept into my thoughts, accompanied by a flicker of worry. Had something unexpected come up? Was he caught in a situation that demanded his attention?

I pushed aside the rising anxiety, reminding myself that Az was more than capable of handling whatever challenges arose. Still, a part of me longed for his presence, for the familiar reassurance that he brought. The bond we shared, forged through trials and shared experiences, had grown stronger with each passing day. His absence left an emptiness in the room, a void that I struggled to fill.

With a sigh, I shifted on the sofa, adjusting the makeshift bandage on my hand. The dull pain served as a constant reminder of the day's events, of the struggles I had faced and the battles that lay ahead. I knew that my journey in this realm was far from over, and that every challenge was a stepping stone toward proving my worth.

As I waited, I allowed my thoughts to drift to the memories we had created together—the moments of laughter, shared stories, and stolen glances that had woven a connection between us. Az had become a steadfast presence in my life, a beacon of support and understanding in a world that often felt foreign and daunting.

But as the minutes turned into hours, the reality of his absence settled in. A mixture of worry and frustration began to gnaw at me, urging me to take action. Pushing aside the worry, I let the darkness consume me.

The next day dawned, casting a feeble light into the chamber. Despite the restless night, I had managed to gather my resolve, pushing aside the consuming worry that had threatened to engulf me. Determination was my ally, and I refused to let the darkness take hold.

As I entered Prince Kael's chamber once more, I focused on the task at hand—changing the bed covers with precision and efficiency. The morning sunlight filtered through the curtains, casting a warm glow that illuminated the room. The familiar routine provided a semblance of normalcy amidst the tumultuous emotions that churned within me.

Engrossed in my work, I hardly noticed the passage of time until a soft sound caught my attention. Startled, I turned my gaze toward the open bathroom door, and my heart skipped a beat.

There, emerging from the steam-filled room, stood Prince Kael—his damp hair tousled, water droplets glistening on his bare chest and shoulders. A towel was loosely draped around his waist, hanging dangerously low, and my breath caught in my throat.

My cheeks flushed with a mixture of surprise and embarrassment as I quickly averted my gaze, my heart racing at the unexpected sight. My mind raced, struggling to compose itself as I focused on my task, my fingers working mechanically to smooth the new bedspread over the mattress.

"Good morning, Elvira," his voice greeted, the casual tone contrasting with the flustered emotions that coursed through me.

I cleared my throat, my cheeks still tinged with pink, and managed to respond, "Good morning, Your Highness."

I dared a glance in his direction, my gaze inadvertently meeting his. Prince Kael's lips quirked into a half-smile, his expression carrying a hint of amusement that only served to intensify my embarrassment.

"Did I catch you at an inopportune moment?" he asked, his tone light and teasing.

My cheeks grew hotter, and I shook my head, determined to maintain my composure. "No, Your Highness. I was simply in the midst of changing the bed covers."

He chuckled softly, a sound that sent a shiver down my spine. "Ah, I see. Well, do carry on then."

I nodded, my fingers trembling slightly as I smoothed out the last wrinkle in the fabric. It was a battle to keep my focus on the task, to ignore the presence of the prince mere feet away from me, his proximity both exhilarating and unnerving.

I nodded, my fingers trembling slightly as I smoothed out the last wrinkle in the fabric. It was a battle to keep my focus on the task, to ignore the presence of the prince mere feet away from me, his proximity both exhilarating and unnerving. The air seemed charged with an unspoken tension, and I couldn't help but steal a few glances in his direction as I worked.

Suddenly, Prince Kael's voice broke through the silence, drawing my attention. "Elvira."

I turned, my heart skipping a beat as I met his gaze. His expression was different now, his eyes fixed on something other than the bed covers. My heart raced as I followed his line of sight, realizing that he had noticed my uncovered burnt hand.

He stepped closer, his gaze shifting from my eyes to my hand. Without a word, he gently reached out, his touch surprisingly gentle as his fingers closed around my injured hand. I watched, a mixture of surprise and curiosity swirling within me, as he guided me to sit on the edge of the bed.

"Sit," he commanded softly, his voice carrying an unusual note of concern.

I complied, settling onto the bed as he knelt before me, his attention solely on my burnt hand. His touch was careful and deliberate, and I couldn't help but feel a strange sense of vulnerability as he tended to my injury.

He studied the burn, his brows furrowing slightly in concentration. "This should have healed by now," he murmured, more to himself than to me.

I hesitated for a moment before responding, my voice a mixture of uncertainty and explanation. "Well, you see, humans don't possess... magical abilities to heal like demons do."

He looked up, genuine confusion in his eyes. "Magical abilities?"

"Yes, I believe that is what I said."

He continued to tend to my hand, his touch surprisingly gentle as he applied a soothing salve. His expression was thoughtful, contemplative, as if processing the information I had just shared.

"So," he began, his voice a low murmur, "your kind is devoid of such inherent powers?"

I sighed softly, leaning back slightly against the bed as I considered his question. "Yes, that's correct. We don't possess any magical gifts. Our healing is a slower, natural process."

Prince Kael's fingers continued their ministrations, his touch sending a tingling sensation through my skin. I couldn't help but feel a mixture of emotions—gratitude, surprise, and a growing sense of connection that defied the barriers between our worlds. I feel like a machosist.

As he focused on my burnt hand, his brow furrowed in concentration, I found my gaze drawn to his chest. It was a fleeting glimpse, a hint of vulnerability that contrasted sharply with his usual façade of authority and power. There, just above the curve of his towel, a scar stretched across his chest, its path tracing a line down to his belly button.

Intrigued and curious, I hesitated for a moment before my fingers moved of their own accord. The scar held a story, a narrative that I yearned to uncover. It was a glimpse into his past, a glimpse into the battles he had fought, the challenges he had endured. It was a chance to see beneath the surface, to understand the man behind the prince.

Without fully realizing what I was doing, I reached out tentatively, my fingers grazing the edge of the scar. The touch was light, barely there, and yet it felt like a connection—a bridge between two worlds that were meant to be separate. I traced the scar's path, my touch feather-light as I followed its journey.

But just as my fingers grazed the scar, an unexpected tension filled the air. Prince Kael's grip on my hand suddenly tightened, his fingers biting into my skin with a force that startled me. My gaze shot up to meet his, and what I saw in his eyes sent a shiver down my spine.

His expression had changed, his features hardening into a mask of coldness. The warmth that had momentarily softened his demeanor was gone, replaced by an unsettling intensity. The atmosphere in the room shifted, the connection we had briefly shared replaced by an insurmountable distance.

"Enough," he growled, his voice cutting through the air like a blade. His grip on my hand remained unrelenting, a silent warning that left my heart racing. "You will not touch what does not belong to you."

His words were sharp, his tone laced with a potent mixture of anger and command. I swallowed hard, a lump forming in my throat as I struggled to comprehend the sudden change in his behavior. The room that had once felt like a place of curiosity and connection had transformed into a battleground, a place of tension and uncertainty.

I tried to pull my hand away, but his grip only tightened further. The pain was sharp, a physical reminder of the power he held over me. I met his gaze, my eyes wide with a mixture of fear and confusion. "Prince Kael," I stammered, my voice shaky, "you're hurting me."

His grip loosened slightly, his fingers releasing their vice-like hold on my hand. But his gaze remained cold, unyielding. "Leave," he commanded, his voice dripping with ice. "Leave my chambers at once."

The shift was jarring, the abruptness of his change in demeanor leaving me disoriented. I stood up slowly, my injured hand cradled against my chest, my heart heavy with a mixture of emotions. The sense of connection that had briefly bloomed between us had withered in an instant, replaced by a wall of hostility and distance.

As I walked through the corridor, the sharp scream of anger pierced the air, causing me to startle. Turning toward the source of the commotion, I saw a scene that I hadn't anticipated. There, in all her resplendent beauty, was a princess, her features twisted with fury as she unleashed her frustration on an unfortunate servant.

Her golden hair cascaded down her shoulders like a waterfall of sunlight, framing a face that could have belonged to a goddess. Her eyes blazed with a fire that matched the intensity of her voice, her demands ringing through the corridor with an air of entitlement. She was a vision of regal elegance, and yet her demeanor was anything but dignified.

I hesitated, my steps faltering as I inadvertently became a spectator to her tantrum. It was a spectacle that I hadn't expected to witness, and I found myself frozen in place, unsure of how to proceed. But as fate would have it, my momentary lapse did not go unnoticed.

The princess's gaze snapped in my direction, her eyes narrowing as they locked onto mine. For a heartbeat, time seemed to stand still as our eyes met, and in that instant, I saw recognition flicker in her gaze. It was as though she had singled me out from the sea of faces, her focus zeroing in on the unfamiliar servant who had dared to witness her outburst.

Before I could react, she was moving toward me, her steps purposeful and deliberate. Her expression remained a mask of anger, her delicate features contorted with a potent mixture of rage and superiority. As she closed the distance between us, her eyes never left mine, and I found myself involuntarily holding my breath.

And then, without warning, her hand shot out, her fingers closing around a strand of my hair. The sudden pull sent a jolt of pain through my scalp, and I winced, unable to suppress the reaction. She tugged at my hair, her grip unrelenting, and I felt a sharp pang of both surprise and indignation.

"Are you blind as well as incompetent?" she hissed, her voice dripping with venom. "Is it so difficult to do one simple task properly?"

I swallowed hard, my heart racing as I tried to find my voice. "I apologize, Your Highness," I managed, my tone respectful despite the seething anger that simmered beneath the surface. "I did not mean to intrude or—"

"Silence!" she snapped, her grip on my hair tightening even further. The pain was intense, a stark reminder of her authority and my position as a servant. "I have no use for your pathetic excuses. You will do well to remember your place."

As the seconds ticked by, her anger seemed to intensify, her frustration pouring out in a torrent of words that were both cutting and cruel. It was a verbal assault, a tirade that left me reeling, my pride wounded and my patience tested to its limits. But even as her words continued to wash over me, I refused to meet her aggression with defiance. I held my gaze steady, my eyes locked onto hers, a silent testament to the strength that lay beneath the surface.

Finally, after what felt like an eternity, she released her grip on my hair with a contemptuous shove. I stumbled back slightly, my fingers instinctively moving to soothe the sore spot on my scalp. She regarded me with a mixture of disdain and triumph, as though she had proven her dominance over an insignificant peon.

"Remember this," she spat, her voice dripping with scorn. "One more mistake, and I'll make sure you regret ever setting foot in this palace."

Her words hung in the air like a chilling promise, a threat that carried the weight of her authority and the consequences that awaited any misstep. The remnants of her fury seemed to linger around me, a constant reminder of the delicate balance I had to maintain in this intricate dance of servitude.

With a nod that conveyed both acknowledgment and deference, I replied, "Of course, Your Highness. I will see to it that your clothes and hair are prepared to your satisfaction."

As she turned away, her regal demeanor seemingly restored, I took a moment to collect myself. The task ahead was clear, and I had no room for error. I moved with purpose, my steps swift and efficient, as I made my way to her chambers.

Entering the opulent space, I was met with an array of luxurious fabrics, exquisite garments fit for royalty. My fingers deftly selected the ensemble that would best suit her preferences and the occasion, laying out each piece with meticulous care. Her wardrobe was a testament to her elevated status, a reminder of the world she inhabited, and the demands that came with it.

Next came the task of tending to her hair—a task that required both skill and precision. I gathered the necessary tools and accessories, arranging them neatly on a nearby table. The mirror before me reflected a reflection that felt almost surreal—a servant amidst the splendor of a princess's chambers, tasked with the responsibility of ensuring her appearance was flawless.

As I worked, my focus remained unwavering, my hands moving with practiced ease. I braided, twisted, and arranged her hair, each strand a canvas on which I carefully crafted an intricate design. It was a silent artistry, a creation that spoke volumes despite the absence of words.

Finally, I stepped back to admire my work. The hairstyle was elegant and sophisticated, befitting her status. With a sense of accomplishment, I approached the array of clothing, selecting the chosen attire that would complete her ensemble. The fabrics flowed like liquid silk, the craftsmanship evident in every seam and stitch.

Presenting the completed ensemble to her, I awaited her inspection, my demeanor composed and respectful.

Her scrutinizing gaze felt like a weight upon me as I stood there, waiting for her assessment. Her silence stretched, and I could sense the tension building in the room. And then, with a sudden, furious motion, she snatched the hairbrush from the table.

Before I could react, the hairbrush was hurtling through the air, a missile of frustration and anger. My reflexes kicked in, and I instinctively raised my arm to shield myself. The impact stung, and I felt a searing pain as the bristles of the brush struck my skin. A hiss escaped me, a mixture of surprise and pain, as I instinctively cradled the stinging area.

Her voice cut through the silence, dripping with disdain. "Disgusting," she spat, her tone a venomous indictment of my efforts. "You dare to present this to me?"

My heart raced, a whirlwind of emotions churning within me. The pain in my arm was nothing compared to the hurt that pierced through me at her words. To have my hard work dismissed so callously, to be deemed inadequate in her eyes—it was a blow to both my pride and my resilience.

"I-I apologize, Your Highness," I managed, my voice steadying despite the turmoil within. "If it does not meet your expectations, I will make the necessary adjustments."

A mirthless laugh escaped her lips, a sound that carried a cruel edge. "Adjustments? There is no saving this disaster," she declared, her gaze cold and unyielding.

With a sense of defeat, I began to gather the items strewn across the table, my movements mechanical as I struggled to hold onto my composure. Her words had wounded me, and yet I knew that I had to endure—to prove that I was capable of rising above her contempt.

As I turned to leave, her voice rang out once more, a final command that cut deeper than any blade. "Get out," she ordered, her voice a harsh dismissal.

I nodded, my eyes downcast, as I retreated from the chamber. The door closed behind me, a barrier between myself and the storm that raged within those opulent walls. The corridor outside felt like a refuge, a sanctuary from the weight of her expectations and the venom of her scorn.

I leaned against the cool stone wall, my breath shaky as I processed the encounter. The throbbing pain in my arm was a tangible reminder of the price I had paid for daring to enter her world—to strive for excellence amidst the chaos of her demands.

But even as the pain pulsed through my bruised skin, a fire ignited within me—a fire that refused to be extinguished by her cruelty. I would not let her disdain define me. I would not allow her words to erode the determination that had carried me this far.

With a deep, steadying breath, I pushed away from the wall and straightened my posture. The path ahead was not an easy one, but I was resolved to navigate it with grace, resilience, and an unwavering commitment to my own worth.

Chapter 17

As I scrubbed the dishes in the corner of the kitchen, my ears pricked up at the sound of hushed whispers from the other servants nearby. The name "Auzrael" caught my attention, and I couldn't help but eavesdrop on their conversation. They were discussing Princess Isabel's latest tantrum, fueled by the fact that Auzrael was away attending to his royal duties in another kingdom.

"He's always been there to serve her every whim," one servant remarked with a hint of annoyance. "I can't believe she's throwing such a fit just because he's not here for a few days."

Another servant chimed in, "Well, she's used to having him at her beck and call. They've always been so close, you know."

I felt a pang of jealousy and longing as I listened to them talk about Auzrael's closeness to Princess Isabel. I knew their bond was strong, but it still hurt to hear how much she relied on him, especially when I wished he would rely on me too.

"He's probably off gallivanting with some other beautiful woman," a third servant remarked, a touch of bitterness in her voice.

"Who knows," another added with a shrug. "All I know is, she's in a terrible mood, and it's not going to be pleasant for anyone around her."

I tried to focus on my task, pushing away the twinge of jealousy and insecurity that threatened to consume me. Auzrael had never explicitly confessed his feelings for me, and we had decided to take things slow, but that didn't stop me from hoping that one day we could be more than just friends and confidants.

As the day wore on, the chatter of the servants continued, and the gossip about Princess Isabel and Auzrael's absence persisted. I couldn't help but wonder what Auzrael was doing in that distant kingdom. Was he thinking of me as I thought of him? Did he miss me as much as I missed him?

As the sun began to set, I found myself standing by the window of the kitchen, lost in my thoughts. The sky was painted in hues of orange and pink, a beautiful backdrop to the turmoil of emotions within me. It was in moments like these that I allowed myself to admit the depth of my feelings for Auzrael, even if it remained unspoken between us.

In the quiet solitude of the kitchen, I allowed myself to daydream about the possibility of a future with him—a future where we could openly acknowledge our love for each other, a future where we could be together without fear of judgment or consequence.

As I turned around, I faced Prince Kael, my heart skipped a beat, and I felt a rush of conflicting emotions. The sight of him, with his smirking lips and piercing eyes, sent a surge of adrenaline through me, even though I tried to deny the attraction that seemed to be blossoming within. My heart belonged to Auzrael, and I had to remind myself of that fact, even as my body betrayed my mind.

He taunted me, claiming that I was slacking off, and a mixture of irritation and embarrassment flared within me. I knew I had been diligently working, but there was little point in arguing with him. His words had a way of getting under my skin, and I had learned that it was best to keep my composure in his presence.

"What do you want, Prince Kael?" I asked, trying to maintain a tone of neutrality.

He smirked, seemingly amused by my persistence. "Follow me," he commanded, his eyes locking onto mine with an intensity that made my heart flutter.

"Why should I?" I retorted, my frustration getting the better of me.

Kael's lips curved into a wicked grin. "Curiosity, perhaps?" he teased, his voice a low, seductive murmur. "Or maybe you just can't resist the opportunity to be in my presence."

I felt my cheeks flush, both from irritation and the inexplicable attraction I felt toward him. "I have more important things to do than follow you around," I replied, trying to sound unaffected.

He raised an eyebrow, his eyes scanning me from head to toe. "Oh, I'm sure you do," he remarked, his tone tinged with conde-scension. "But I do believe you'll find my company much more entertaining than scrubbing dishes."

I hesitated for a moment, torn between my duty and my curiosity. A part of me was intrigued by what he wanted, even though I knew it was probably best to keep my distance from him. But there was something about his aura that drew me in, an air of mystery that I couldn't resist.

"Fine," I conceded, trying to maintain a facade of indifference. "Lead the way."

He turned and walked down the corridor, and I followed, my heart pounding in my chest. I couldn't help but wonder what he had in mind, and I tried to push away the fluttering feeling in my stomach. My heart belonged to Auzrael, and I had to remind myself of that fact.

As we reached his room, he opened the door and gestured for me to enter. I stepped inside cautiously, my senses on high alert. Kael closed the door behind us, and I couldn't help but feel a sense of trepidation. What was he planning?

He turned to face me, his expression inscrutable. "Do you know why I asked you to come here?" he asked, his voice low and measured.

I shook my head, trying to quell the nervousness that was bubbling within me. "No, I don't," I replied honestly.

A small smirk played on his lips. "I wanted to see how you would react," he admitted, his eyes searching mine for any sign of vulnerability.

I raised an eyebrow, my curiosity piqued. "React to what?"

"To me," he stated boldly, taking a step closer to me.

I felt a jolt of electricity shoot through me, and I took a step back, trying to put some distance between us. "What do you mean?" I asked, my voice trembling slightly.

He chuckled, seemingly amused by my discomfort. "You're different from the other servants," he said, his eyes never leaving mine. "You're not afraid to challenge me, to stand up to me. I find that intriguing."

I swallowed hard, trying to process his words. It was true that I hadn't been afraid to speak my mind in front of him, but that was because I knew he wouldn't retaliate against me like he did with others. But did that mean he was attracted to me? The thought seemed absurd, and yet, there was a glint in his eyes that made me wonder.

"You're a puzzle, Elvira," he continued, his voice dropping to a whisper. "And I'm curious to see what lies beneath the surface."

I felt a surge of conflicting emotions, unsure of how to respond to his boldness. My heart was reserved for Auzrael, and I couldn't let myself be swayed by Kael's charm. But there was an undeniable pull between us, an unspoken connection that seemed to transcend the boundaries of our worlds.

Before I could respond, Kael leaned in, his lips dangerously close to mine. My heart raced, and I instinctively took a step back, my mind screaming at me to resist. But in that moment, all I could feel was the magnetic pull between us, a desire that I couldn't explain.

He moves towards my ear and whispers, "Can you stitch?"

"Stitch?" I repeated, taken aback by his question, "Why are you asking about stitching?"

Kael's gaze flickered with an unreadable emotion, and for a moment, I thought he might brush off the question. He lifted his powerful arms, and removed his shirt. Kael's bare chest was a sight to behold, a canvas that told stories of battles fought and scars earned. His skin was a rich, dusky shade, smooth and adorned with the marks of his demon heritage. The play of shadows and light over his chiseled muscles accentuated every contour, giving him an aura of strength and power.

His broad shoulders and well-defined pectorals spoke of a demon accustomed to physical prowess, while his lean waistline hinted at agility and grace. The scars that crisscrossed his chest and abdomen told tales of past encounters, each mark a reminder of his resilience and determination.

His chest rose and fell with every breath, and I found myself drawn to the rhythmic movement, captivated by the raw masculinity that emanated from him. The absence of a healing wound across his upper abdomen seemed puzzling, and it added an air of vulnerability to his otherwise imposing presence.

His eyes, framed by long, dark lashes, held a depth that was both intriguing and mysterious. In that moment of vulnerability, I saw a side of him that he rarely showed to the world—a glimpse of the person behind the prince, with layers of complexity waiting to be unraveled.

Kael cockily asks, "Enjoying the view?"

I quickly averted my gaze, trying to focus on the task at hand.

"I'm merely attending to your wound, Your Highness," I replied, my tone steady despite the roiling emotions inside me.

Kael smirked, his eyes gleaming with amusement. "Of course," he said with a knowing glint in his eyes. "Though I must say, not many get the privilege to see me like this."

I resisted the urge to roll my eyes, refusing to indulge his cocky demeanor. "I'm sure," I retorted, keeping my focus on the task at hand.

"Be gentle," Kael remarked, his voice tinged with a hint of amusement. "It stings a bit."

"I'll do my best," I replied, my voice steady despite the rush of nerves I felt. As I inspected the wound, I saw that it was a long gash that extended from across his ribcage. The skin around it was angry and inflamed, evidence of a wound that had stubbornly refused to heal.

"You're a demon," I blurted out without thinking, my curiosity getting the better of me. "Shouldn't this have healed by now?"

Kael's expression darkened, a shadow passing over his features.

I hesitated for a moment before gently prodding the wound, trying to understand its nature. "Does it hurt?" I asked, my concern for his well-being overriding my earlier irritation.

He winced slightly at the touch, his jaw clenching for a moment before he composed himself. "No," he replied tersely. "But it's a constant reminder."

I felt a pang of sympathy for him, wondering what could have caused such a wound and why it refused to heal. But I knew better than to pry into his personal affairs, especially considering our complicated relationship as prince and servant.

Finishing stitching the wound, I carefully covered the wound with a clean bandage, trying to make him as comfortable as possible. "You should try to take it easy," I advised, my instincts taking over.

Kael chuckled softly, a hint of bitterness in his voice. "Easy isn't really my style," he remarked, his eyes meeting mine in a moment of shared understanding.

I nodded in acknowledgment, realizing that Kael was a prince burdened with responsibilities and expectations that I could never fully comprehend. Despite his cocky demeanor, there was a vulnerability in him that spoke of a deeper struggle.

Kael's eyes lingered on the bruise on my arm, a frown creasing his forehead. "What happened to your arm?" he asked, his voice surprisingly gentle.

I glanced down at the bruise, feeling a bit self-conscious. "It's nothing," I replied, trying to brush it off. "Just a small accident while I was working."

But Kael wasn't easily deterred. He stepped closer, his eyes searching mine for any sign of discomfort. "Are you sure?" he pressed, concern evident in his tone. "It looks painful."

I shifted uncomfortably under his gaze, feeling a mix of gratitude and unease at his sudden concern for me. "It's really fine," I insisted, trying to downplay the significance of the bruise. "I've had worse."

He seemed unconvinced, his gaze lingering on the bruise for a moment longer, instead of letting me go he made me sit on the chair. Kael's touch was surprisingly gentle as he tended to my bruise, his fingers tracing a soothing path over the discolored skin. I couldn't help but feel a sense of vulnerability in that moment, allowing him to see a side of me that I rarely showed to others.

"It's just a small bruise," I said, my voice softer than I intended, "I've had worse."

He looked up at me, his gaze unwavering. "It doesn't mean it shouldn't be taken care of," he replied, his voice firm yet gentle. "You shouldn't have to endure unnecessary pain."

I couldn't deny the truth in his words, and for a moment, I let myself lean into his touch, finding a measure of comfort in his presence. It was a strange juxtaposition—to feel both drawn to and wary of someone at the same time.

As he tended to my bruise, his eyes drifted to my burnt hand, and a flicker of guilt crossed his features.

My heart skipped a beat as I noticed the guilt in Kael's eyes. A rush of mixed emotions swept through me—confusion, anger, and an unexpected wave of empathy. I knew that accidents happened, but it was hard to ignore the fact that he had caused the burn on my hand.

His grip on my hand tightened, the weight of his apology hanging in the air between us. It was a vulnerable moment, and I found myself conflicted once again. Part of me wanted to pull away, to maintain a distance from him, but another part of me felt a strange sense of connection and understanding.

"I forgive you," I said finally, my voice barely above a whisper.

He just nodded and left the room. As I left Kael's room once again, I couldn't shake the feeling that our paths were destined to cross again. There was something about him—something that both intrigued and unnerved me. But no matter the pull I felt, I knew that my heart belonged to another.

In the quiet moments of the night, as I lay in Auzrael's chamber, I thought about the choices that lay before me. The demon prince had captured my heart, and I knew that my love for him was undeniable. But with Kael's presence lingering in the back of my mind, I couldn't help but question the complexities of my own emotions.

As I stood in the presence of Behomath, early in the morning, his words sent a mixture of confusion and unease rippling through me. The morning light filtered through the windows, casting a soft glow on the scene unfolding before me. He had ordered me to shift to the servant's quaters due to Auzrael's fiancée's arrival. The demon's instructions were clear, but the implications of his words left me taken aback.

"A new wardrobe for you," he stated, his voice devoid of any emotion as he presented the collection of outfits to me. I couldn't help but notice the skimpy and revealing nature of the clothes he had chosen. It was as if he intended to strip away any sense of modesty or comfort that I had managed to hold onto.

My gaze shifted from Behomath to the clothes in my hands, and a mixture of emotions swirled within me. On one hand, I felt a surge of anger and indignation. It was as if my identity and dignity were being stripped away along with my old clothes. On the other hand, there was a growing sense of unease and vulnerability. The thought of wearing these outfits made me feel exposed, as if I were being forced to reveal parts of myself that I wasn't ready to share.

I took a deep breath, my fingers tightening around the fabric of one of the outfits. "Why?" I asked, my voice steady despite the turmoil within me. "Why am I being given these clothes?"

Behomath's eyes bore into mine, a glint of something unreadable in his gaze. "The demon court has its expectations," he replied cryptically. "As a servant here, you are subject to the rules and orders of your superiors."

The weight of his words settled heavily on my shoulders, and I realized that I was caught in a world that I didn't fully understand—a world where I had to navigate not only the politics of the demon court but also the expectations that came with my position.

Still, I refused to let go of my sense of self and dignity. My fingers clenched around the fabric of the clothes, and I looked up at Behomath with a determination that surprised even me. "I won't wear these," I stated firmly.

A flicker of something akin to annoyance crossed his features, but he remained composed. "You have little choice in the matter," he replied. "These are the clothes that have been chosen for you by the prince himself, and you will wear them while you serve him."

I met his gaze with a defiant glare. "I am serving him, not pleasuring him."

As Behomath's eyes narrowed, his patience seemingly wearing thin, a new presence entered the scene. I turned to see Kael stepping into the room, his presence commanding attention as he surveyed the situation with a raised eyebrow.

"What seems to be the matter here?" Kael's voice cut through the tense air, his tone a blend of curiosity and authority.

Behomath's gaze shifted to Kael, his expression shifting slightly as he acknowledged the prince's presence. "Prince Kael," he greeted with a nod. "I was simply delivering the new wardrobe to Elvira, as instructed."

Kael's eyes flickered to the clothes in my hands, and then back to Behomath. "I see," he said, his voice carrying a hint of skepticism. "And why does it seem like there's a disagreement?"

I took a deep breath, the weight of the situation heavy on my shoulders. "These clothes," I began, my voice steady despite the tension in the room, "they're going to restrict my ability to work. I am not a hooker but a servant, Prince Kael, I would like to remind you of my position in the 'Royal court' that all of you like reminding me."

Kael's gaze remained focused on me, his expression inscrutable as he absorbed my words. There was a pause, a charged silence that hung between us as his brows furrowed slightly.

"Very well," he finally said, his voice calm and measured. "If you find these clothes hindering your ability to work, you're welcome to work without any clothes."

My eyes widened in surprise at his response, my heart pounding in my chest. The audacity of his suggestion caught me off guard, and I felt a flush of indignation rise to my cheeks.

"I—what?" I stammered, my mind struggling to process his words.

Kael's lips quirked in a half-smile, his gaze holding mine without flinching. "You said the clothes would restrict your work. I'm offering a solution. If clothes are the issue, eliminate them altogether."

I'll take your 'clothes'," I grunted out, holding back my tongue.

Kael's lips twitched into a half-smile, his tone dripping with sarcasm. "Ah, so that's how you get things done, Behomath."

Behomath's eyes narrowed, a mixture of annoyance and resignation crossing his features. "Yes, your highness," he muttered, his tone begrudging.

My eyes shifted between the two, the tension in the room palpable. Kael's playful sarcasm seemed to cut through the weight of the situation, offering a moment of levity that contrasted with Behomath's stern demeanor.

Behomath's gaze flickered to me, his expression softening slightly. "Just do your job, girl, and let's not make a spectacle of everything."

I nodded, a flicker of understanding passing between us. Despite his brusque exterior, Behomath's words held a trace of concern, a reminder that navigating the intricacies of the demon court required a careful balance of defiance and discretion.

Chapter 18

I stood in the corridor, arranging the flowers in the vases and replacing the water in them. I turned my head up, upon hearing footsteps. My heart leaped in my chest as I spotted Az walking down the corridor, his presence a beacon of familiarity and comfort. A genuine smile graced my lips, excitement surging through me as I took a step forward to greet him.

But before I could even utter a word, a sudden commotion drew my attention. My smile faltered as my gaze shifted, my heart sinking like a stone in my chest. Princess Isabel, the same woman who tortured me with her tantrums the past two days, pounced on Az, her arms encircling his neck as she pressed her lips to his.

Time seemed to stand still as I watched the unexpected display of affection unfold before me. My breath caught in my throat, a mixture of surprise, disbelief, and a twinge of jealousy washing over me. The embrace felt intimate, possessive, and a pang of something I didn't quite want to acknowledge clenched at my heart.

For a moment, I was frozen in place, an outsider looking in on a scene that I had never anticipated. The corridor felt like a tunnel, my presence invisible as their connection intensified before me. I was painfully aware of my position as a mere servant, a silent observer to a world that was not mine to navigate.

For a moment, I was frozen in place, an outsider looking in on a scene that I had never anticipated. The corridor felt like a tunnel, my presence invisible as their connection intensified before me. I was painfully aware of my position as a mere servant, a silent observer to a world that was not mine to navigate.

Unable to bear the sight any longer, I turned around swiftly, my heart aching with an unfamiliar mix of emotions. I took hurried steps away from them, each footfall echoing the turmoil within me. My mind was a whirlwind of thoughts, a storm of confusion and longing that I struggled to make sense of.

As I walked, the corridor seemed to stretch endlessly before me, a path that led nowhere and everywhere all at once. I couldn't shake the image of their embrace from my mind—the intimacy, the closeness, the unspoken understanding that existed between them. It was a realm I had never ventured into, a realm that reminded me of the boundaries that separated us.

Lost in my thoughts, I rounded a corner, only to collide with someone unexpectedly. The impact sent a jolt of surprise through me, and I stumbled back slightly, a gasp escaping my lips. Before me stood Kael, his presence as striking and imposing as ever.

Tears welled in my eyes, my emotions spilling over despite my best efforts to contain them. The loneliness I had carried, the weight of my own struggles, suddenly felt overwhelming in his presence.

He reached out, his fingers brushing against my cheek in a gesture that was surprisingly gentle. "Who hurt you?," he asked, his voice a soothing murmur. He pulled me into his room, and locked the door behind him.

Before I could fully comprehend my own actions, a surge of emotion compelled me to close the distance between us. I pressed my lips against his. His lips were soft and warm against mine, a juxtaposition to the turmoil that raged within me.

My fingers found their way to his hair, tangling in the dark strands as I pulled him closer, needing to feel the depth of his presence. Kael's arms encircled me, his touch both possessive and gentle, as if he was determined to shield me from the world's harsh realities. His large hands tightened on my waist, The gentle kiss turned demanding wanting every inch of my body. This feels so wrong and right at the same time. I shouldn't be betraying Auzrael like this, but yet I couldn't stop myself from pulling away. I could feel Kael caressing my skin, He tugged my skirt up, I felt his handing squeezing my left cheek, I moaned into his mouth.

I arched my back and grinding myself onto him wanting him to please me. His mouth found it's way to my neck, teasing the skin, he sucks onto it while his fingers work their way into pussy, He slowly tortures me, he rubs his long, thick finger over my clit, adding the exact amount of please. He tugs my chest and lets my breasts out. He gives attention to my hard nipples that are hard and swollen, begging for attention. His mouth makes it way lower, He tugs my nipple with his teeth, a surge of pain flows through my body, just as he tugs it harder, he sucks onto the nipple. I let out a whine as he goes back to sucking and licking the other nipple. While he latches himself onto my boobs, he slips a finger into my cunt.

"You are fucking, soaking, Elvira." He growls.

"Please." I whine.

His finger pumps in and out in a rhythm. I cry out in pleasure.

"I'm going to cum." I say panting as he sucks the skin of my upper left breast.

I cried out while I orgasmed on his fingers and a pain shot out on my neck. As I brought my hand to my neck to soothe the sudden pang of pain, I felt a cool, tingling sensation spread across my skin. Confusion clouded my thoughts, and I instinctively turned to Kael, seeking an explanation for this unexpected sensation.

Before I could voice my question, his eyes widened in realization, his gaze fixated on my neck. His lips parted, but no words emerged. Instead, he reached out tentatively, his fingers brushing against my skin, tracing the area where the sensation had originated.

My heart raced as I followed his gaze downward, my hand now resting over my left chest. And that's when I saw it—a smear of blood. My eyes widened in shock, my fingers trembling as I touched the dampness on my skin. It was unmistakable; the cool sensation, the pain, the blood—the fucker bit me.

I turned to Kael, my eyes searching his for any semblance of an explanation. But his expression remained unreadable, a mask that revealed nothing of his intentions. My voice shook as I finally managed to speak, my words a mixture of confusion and urgency.

"You bit me," I said, my voice barely a whisper. It was as if the reality of the mark had cemented itself in my mind, and I couldn't escape the weight of what had just transpired.

Kael's response was surprising—a nonchalant shrug of his shoulders. "It's just a mark," he said, his tone dismissive. "It'll fade away."

I couldn't believe the casual way he was treating this situation. It was as if the significance of the mark was lost on him. My frustration grew, and I couldn't hold back the barrage of questions that tumbled from my lips.

"What mark?" I asked, my voice tinged with a mixture of confusion and anger. "And why did you do it? What does it mean?"

Kael's gaze met mine, his expression still composed but his eyes held a flicker of something I couldn't quite decipher. "It's a bond mark," he explained, his tone matter-of-fact. "A mark that signifies a connection, a mate bond. It's meant to strengthen the ties between demons, to forge a deeper connection between two individuals."

I blinked, my mind racing to comprehend the implications of his words. A bond mark—a connection that went beyond the physical, a tie that bound two souls together. It was a concept that seemed foreign to me, yet its weight settled heavily in my chest.

"But why?" I asked, my voice barely above a whisper. "Why mark me? What purpose does it serve?"

Kael's expression softened, his eyes meeting mine with an intensity that sent a shiver down my spine. "The mark is only permanent if the bond is real," he said, his voice surprisingly gentle. "If two individuals are true mates, the mark becomes a permanent symbol of their connection. But since you're human, you don't have to worry about that."

His words offered a strange mix of relief and confusion. Relief that the mark might fade, that its permanence wasn't set in stone. But confusion because I couldn't ignore the complexity of the situation. I wasn't just dealing with the aftermath of being marked; I was grappling with the tangled web of emotions that connected me to Kael in ways I couldn't fully understand.

"True mates?" I repeated, the words feeling foreign on my tongue. "What does that even mean?"

Kael's gaze held mine, his expression a mixture of somber reflection. "It means that two individuals are destined to be together," he explained. "Their souls are intertwined, and the bond mark becomes a physical representation of that connection. But like I said, that's not something you need to worry about. Humans and demons don't form true mate bonds. There might be exceptions but it won't be like that with us."

Kael's words hung in the air like a delicate balance between hope and disappointment. His explanation shed light on a realm of possibilities that I had never considered, and yet, his dismissal of the idea between us stung. I couldn't help but feel a twinge of hurt, a quiet ache that I refused to let show.

"Right," I replied, my voice steady despite the swirl of emotions within me.

Kael's gaze searched mine for a moment, as if he could see beyond the facade I was putting up. There was a tension in the air, an unspoken understanding that we were both navigating uncharted territory. And while his words had provided clarity, they had also opened the door to a realm of questions I wasn't sure I was ready to confront.

He took a step closer, his gaze unwavering. "Elvira," he began, his voice softer now, "I have some work, and I believe that you have your duties to attend to also, if the mark bothers you, let me know."

With a small nod, I turned to leave, my steps carrying me towards the door. But just as I was about to step out, a question that had been nagging at the back of my mind slipped past my lips.

"Kael," I began, my voice hesitant, "should I... cover the mark?"

"Only over the mark and leave the rest," Kael replied, his tone steady. His words carried a hint of amusement, as if he knew that there was more to my concern than just the bond mark itself. I could feel my cheeks warming slightly, a mixture of embarrassment and a surprising sense of camaraderie settling over me.

"Right," I murmured, unable to meet his gaze directly. It was clear that he was well aware of the situation—the hickeys that adorned my neck like an unintended badge of our shared moment. Despite my attempts to appear composed, my body betrayed me with a flush that I couldn't hide.

Kael's lips curved into a faint smile, his expression a blend of understanding and something more difficult to decipher. "Don't worry," he said, his tone casual, "it's not like anyone else will see them. And if they do, well, they'll just have to draw their own conclusions."

His words, while meant to reassure, only seemed to deepen my embarrassment. It was a reminder of the complicated web of secrecy and unspoken emotions that now bound us together. I cleared my throat, my attempt to regain my composure only making me more self-conscious.

As I hurried back to my room, my mind was a whirlwind of conflicting emotions. The encounter with Kael still played in my mind, each word and glance etched vividly. The mark on my chest, the unintended hickeys on my neck, and the complex tangle of feelings that I struggled to make sense of—it was all too much to process.

As I entered the room, my roommate's curious gaze met mine, her eyebrows arching playfully. It didn't take long for her to spot the marks on my neck, and her grin widened mischievously.

"Well, well, what do we have here?" she teased, her voice dripping with amusement.

I sighed inwardly, knowing that there was no escaping her scrutiny. "It's nothing," I replied, my tone casual as I moved towards the mirror, trying to avoid her knowing gaze.

"Nothing?" she repeated, her disbelief evident. "Those certainly look like somethings to me."

I met my own reflection in the mirror, the hickeys stark against my skin. My cheeks warmed with embarrassment, and I quickly moved my hair to partially cover the marks. Anything to divert her attention.

"Seriously, Elvira, spill the beans!" she urged, her curiosity piqued. "Who's the lucky one?"

I hesitated, my mind racing for a plausible explanation. I couldn't exactly tell her the truth—that the marks were from Kael, a prince of the demon realm. The secrecy surrounding our interactions and the depth of emotions I was grappling with were far too complex to share.

"It's just a guard, Sofia," I finally said, my voice carefully neutral. "Someone I've been spending a bit of time with."

Sofia's eyes widened in mock surprise, and she waggled her eyebrows suggestively. "A guard, huh? Well, well, Elvira, you certainly know how to keep things interesting."

I managed a small smile, relieved that my explanation seemed to satisfy her curiosity. At least for now.

"Yeah, just a guard," I repeated, trying to sound nonchalant.

She laughed, the sound light and teasing. "Well, if you ever need any advice on keeping things spicy with your 'guard,' you know where to find me."

I chuckled, appreciating her lightheartedness even as I struggled to reconcile the reality of the situation I found myself in. My roommate's teasing provided a brief respite from the intensity of my thoughts, and for that, I was grateful.

As I settled into my routine for the evening, I couldn't help but steal glances at the mirror, my fingers tracing the faint outline of the bond mark on my chest. It was a reminder of the uncharted territory I now tread, a connection that had formed unexpectedly and left me questioning everything I thought I knew.

And as I lay in bed that night, the mark hidden beneath the fabric of my nightclothes, I wondered about the future that awaited us—a future that seemed uncertain, intriguing, and undeniably entwined.

The next morning, as I prepared to face the day ahead, I found myself standing before the mirror once again. The hickeys on my neck were still there, a testament to the unexpected turn of events that had unfolded. While I had managed to keep the truth hidden from my roommate Sofia, the visible marks were a constant reminder of the secret I now carried.

Sofia was bustling around the room, her cheerful energy a stark contrast to the storm of emotions raging within me. I watched her for a moment, appreciating the distraction she unknowingly provided.

"Sofia," I began, my voice uncertain, "do you think you could help me with something?"

She turned to me with a smile, her eyes curious. "Of course, Elvira! What do you need?"

I hesitated, my fingers lightly touching the hickeys as if to confirm their presence. "It's just... these marks," I said, my voice lowering as embarrassment tinged my cheeks. "I was wondering if you could help me cover them up somehow."

Sofia's gaze shifted to my neck, and her expression shifted from curiosity to understanding. She walked over to me, a reassuring smile on her lips.

"Sure thing," she replied gently. "I can use some makeup to conceal them. No worries, Elvira, I've got your back."

Relief washed over me, gratitude for Sofia's support warming my heart. As she worked on covering the marks, I couldn't help but feel a mixture of emotions. There was a sense of vulnerability in admitting my situation, even to someone as close as Sofia. But her willingness to help, her nonjudgmental demeanor, reminded me that I wasn't alone in this journey.

"Thank you, Sofia," I said softly as she finished her task.

She stepped back, studying her handiwork with a satisfied nod. "No problem at all. Just remember, if you ever need someone to talk to, I'm here."

I smiled, genuinely touched by her kindness. "I appreciate that, really."

With the hickeys now concealed, I felt a weight lift from my shoulders. While the marks were hidden from the world, the complexity of my emotions remained. The connection I shared with Kael, the bond mark on my chest—it was all a reminder of the intricate web that fate had woven around us.

As I went about my day, the memory of Kael's touch lingered, and the undercurrent of emotions continued to simmer beneath the surface. My interactions with him had taken unexpected turns, and while I was navigating uncharted territory, I was determined to face whatever challenges lay ahead.

And as I glanced at the mirror once more before leaving the room, I found a small measure of comfort in the knowledge that I wasn't alone on this journey. With Sofia's friendship and support, I was ready to navigate the intricate dance of secrets, emotions, and the unspoken connection that bound me to Kael—a connection that had the power to reshape both our worlds.

I continued my task, dusting Az's room, a soft cloth in my hand as I gently wiped away the dust that had settled on the various surfaces of Auzrael's room. The room itself held an air of tranquility, a sanctuary amidst the bustling life of the demon kingdom. The muted sunlight filtered through the windows, casting a warm and inviting glow over the furnishings.

As I meticulously went about my work, I was lost in my thoughts, the rhythmic swishing of the cloth a soothing backdrop to my reflections. Auzrael's sudden presence in the room, however, disrupted the peaceful ambiance, causing me to glance up in surprise.

My gaze met his form, clad in his fighting leathers. The sight was a powerful reminder of his dual nature—the prince who walked amongst demons and the fierce warrior who commanded respect. His presence seemed to fill the room, a commanding aura that demanded attention.

"Elvira," he acknowledged with a nod, his voice carrying the weight of his responsibilities and the subtle undercurrent of something deeper.

I lowered my gaze respectfully, my heart quickening ever so slightly at his presence. "Your Highness," I responded, my tone a mixture of respect and familiarity.

"About the incident in the corridor-", Az began explaining, but stopped himself and came closer to me, as though he were sensing something different.

He regarded me for a moment, his eyes narrowing as if he were trying to decipher a hidden truth. "Elvira," he said, his voice low and measured, "there's something... different about you. Have you encountered any trouble?"

I met his gaze, my own curiosity piqued by his words. "Trouble, Your Highness?" I inquired, my brows furrowing slightly.

Auzrael's gaze remained unwavering, his eyes holding a mixture of concern and intrigue. "Elvira," he began, his voice measured, "when you entered the room, I couldn't help but notice a scent... a scent that's not entirely unfamiliar to me."

My heart skipped a beat, a sudden wave of realization washing over me. The incident with Kael in his room, the unexpected closeness that had sparked something within me—it suddenly became clear. Auzrael's keen senses had picked up on the scent, and now I found myself caught in a moment that I had been trying to deny.

"Kael," I whispered, a mixture of apprehension and honesty in my voice.

Auzrael's expression remained composed, but I could sense a depth of understanding in his eyes. "Yes," he confirmed, his tone softening, "Kael's scent lingers on you."

My cheeks flushed with a mixture of embarrassment and vulnerability. It was as if my thoughts had been laid bare, my feelings exposed to the one person who could read me like an open book. Auzrael's perceptiveness was both comforting and unnerving, a reminder that there were no secrets when it came to him.

"I... We were in his room," I stammered, struggling to find the right words to explain the situation. "He helped me with something, and I guess... his scent transferred."

Auzrael's gaze remained steady for a moment, his expression in-scrutable. His silence felt heavy, pregnant with unspoken thoughts and emotions. And then, without a word, he turned and walked out of the room.

I was left standing there, a whirlwind of emotions swirling within me. Doubt, embarrassment, and a touch of regret clouded my mind. I had exposed a part of my world that I had hoped to keep hidden—a world where feelings were tangled, where interactions held layers of meaning that extended beyond mere tasks.

Closing my eyes, I took a deep breath, trying to steady my racing heart. Auzrael's departure had left me feeling vulnerable, as if I had bared my soul and was met with a response that was hard to decipher. I knew he was a prince, burdened with responsibilities and secrets, and yet I couldn't help but wish for a more conclusive interaction, a clearer understanding of where we stood.

As I resumed my duties, the memory of him lingered in my mind.

Chapter 19

As I was settling into sleep, I noticed a dark cloud of shadows staring into me. My heart raced, pounding against my chest like a trapped bird. The world around me shifted, a blur of darkness and disorientation as a strong, cold grip closed around me, wrapping me in an unyielding embrace. Panic clawed at my throat as I tried to scream, my voice caught in my throat as if some invisible force had stolen it away.

The room materialized around me, a stark contrast to the corridors and chambers I had grown accustomed to. Rich velvet fabrics adorned the walls, casting an eerie and opulent glow in the dim light. The bed stood as the centerpiece, its covers smooth and inviting, yet the aura of the room sent shivers down my spine. The shadows seemed to dance with a life of their own, undulating like living entities, twisting and contorting as if they held a willful intent.

Fear clenched my heart, its icy fingers squeezing tight as I struggled to break free from the hold of the shadows. My body felt heavy, as if gravity itself conspired against me. I strained against the invisible restraints, my breaths coming in rapid, shallow gasps.

But the more I fought, the tighter their grip became, until it felt as though the very air had turned against me.

Desperation welled within me, my mind a whirlwind of frantic thoughts. Who—or what—had brought me here? What did they want from me? I strained my ears, hoping to catch the faintest sound, a hint of an explanation. But the silence was suffocating, broken only by the erratic thudding of my heart.

As my attempts to break free grew increasingly futile, a sensation of resignation washed over me. It was as if a realization had dawned: I was powerless in the face of this unseen force. The shadows held dominion over me, their will bending mine to their whim. The fear that had initially gripped me was slowly replaced by a heavy weight of acceptance—an acceptance that I was trapped, at their mercy.

I scanned the room once more, searching for any sign of an exit, any glimmer of hope. But my surroundings seemed to stretch and warp, as though the very space itself defied my attempts to make sense of it. A sickening realization settled within me: this was no ordinary room, no ordinary encounter. It was as if I had been pulled into a realm that defied the laws of the world I knew, a realm where shadows and darkness held sway.

The minutes ticked by, each second stretching into eternity. My heart's frantic rhythm gradually gave way to a numb acceptance, a resignation to the fact that I was trapped, isolated from the world I understood. And as the shadows continued to hold me in their unrelenting grip, a voiceless scream echoed within the confines of my mind—an expression of fear and helplessness that remained unheard, lost in the boundless expanse of darkness.

Just then, a voice broke through the silence, a low and resonant sound that sent shivers down my spine. "Elvira," it called, its tone laced with a potent combination of warmth and longing.

I turned towards the source of the voice, my breath catching in my throat as I saw him—Auzrael. He stood before me, his presence commanding and magnetic. His eyes held mine, a connection that seemed to transcend time and space.

"Welcome," he said, his voice a caress that echoed through the room. "I've brought you here to escape the constraints that bind us in the realm of daylight, to exist in a moment untouched by the outside world."

His words hung in the air, weaving a spell that seemed to draw me closer to him, erasing the boundaries that separated us. But before I could fully surrender to the moment, my instinctive reaction took over. In a mix of surprise and frustration, I slapped his chest, my palm connecting with a resounding smack.

"What the hell, Auzrael!" I exclaimed, my heart still racing from the shock. "You can't just drag me into a room like this without any warning. You scared the living daylights out of me!"

Auzrael's lips curved into a bemused smile, his eyes sparkling with a mixture of amusement and something deeper. "I apologize for the abrupt entrance," he said, his voice laced with a hint of mischief. "I suppose I was eager to share this space with you."

I rolled my eyes, a mixture of annoyance and embarrassment washing over me. "There are better ways to share spaces," I muttered, my cheeks flushing with a mixture of emotions.

He took a step closer, his gaze unwavering. "True," he admitted, his voice softening, "but sometimes, the unexpected can lead to the most memorable experiences."

I crossed my arms, my irritation fading slightly in the face of his earnest expression. "Well, next time, how about a little heads-up?" I retorted, trying to sound more composed than I felt.

Auzrael chuckled, a melodic sound that resonated within the room. "I'll keep that in mind," he replied, his eyes holding mine in a way that was both comforting and exhilarating.

I met his gaze, the intensity of the moment holding me captive. "Well, just remember that I'm not one to be dragged around without warning," I said, a mixture of playfulness and sincerity in my tone.

Auzrael's smile deepened, his fingers trailing along the curve of my jaw. "Noted," he replied, his voice a low murmur that seemed to echo through the room.

"And now that you've slapped me," he remarked, his voice a velvety whisper, "does this mean I've earned a moment to make it up to you?"

I couldn't help but chuckle, the tension that had once gripped me now replaced with a sense of ease. "Well, I suppose it depends on how you plan to make it up to me," I teased, a glint of mischief in my eyes.

Auzrael's gaze held mine, a mixture of desire and tenderness in his depths. "I suppose you'll just have to wait and find out," he replied, his voice a tantalizing promise.

"Close your eyes," he instructed, his words a gentle command.

My heart skipped a beat as Auzrael's fingers gently brushed against my skin, his touch igniting a cascade of sensations that sent shivers down my spine. The air around us seemed charged with an electric tension, anticipation hanging in the air like a fragile thread. I watched as he produced a soft fabric, his intent clear.

"What are you...?" I began, my voice trailing off as he stepped closer, his gaze locking onto mine with an intensity that made my breath catch.

"Trust me," he murmured, his words a soothing caress that seemed to melt away my uncertainty. His fingers worked deftly, securing the blindfold in place, enveloping me in darkness.

At first, all I knew was the absence of light, a deep void that heightened my other senses. The rustling of fabric, the sound of his footsteps—each sensation felt heightened, as though the world had narrowed down to this singular moment.

"Now," Auzrael's voice was a whisper, his presence a reassuring anchor, "breathe."

And then, slowly, Auzrael's fingers brushed against my cheek, his touch a tender caress.

Auzrael's fingers danced lightly across my skin, their touch a teasing caress that sent a shiver down my spine.

"Enjoying the sensation?" he asked, his voice a velvety murmur that seemed to weave around me.

"Yes." I breathed out.

He chuckled softly, the sound like a melody in the air. "You're quite skilled at keeping your emotions in check," he observed, his fingers tracing a path along the curve of my breasts.

"It's a necessary trait for a servant," I replied, a hint of challenge in my voice. His proximity was unsettling, yet I was determined not to let it show.

Auzrael's touch shifted, his fingers brushing against the curve of my waist, his touch warm and lingering. "And what if I told you that sometimes, letting go of control can be quite liberating?"

Auzrael's fingers brushed against the sensitive skin of my inner wrist, his touch sending a jolt of awareness through me. "Tell me, Elvira," he murmured, his voice low and intimate, "have you ever allowed yourself to indulge in something simply because it felt right?" He flipped me on my knees, now my bare ass was arched into the air and was face was resting against the soft covers of the bed.

He leaned in slightly, his breath brushing against my skin. "But sometimes, those choices are the ones that truly define us," his voice a mere breath away.

His touch lingered, his fingers brushing he sensitive skin, "One look at you fucking tits and this gorgeous ass", he says and slaps my cheek making me moan at the contact, "all my blood rushes down to my cock."

"Then let me help you," I whisper, begging him to remove the blind fold. My breasts bounce free and Az's hand was now around them.

His hand slowly moves lower as he explores the valley of my breasts

His touch is cool against my the heat of my body.

"Fuck me," he curses under his breath. One hand sneaks behind my waist as he prompts me to wrap my legs around his waist, bringing that hard part of his in contact with my center.

A whimper escapes me at the sensation, and I can't help myself as I keep rubbing against him. "you're driving me crazy," he says, bending his head and giving one breast a long lick before wrapping his lips around my nipple, sucking it into his mouth.

The warmth of his mouth contrasts with my cold skin, the effect on my body sublime. He follows the contour of my breast, laying small kisses right above the mark of Kael. I was giving into the pleasure and ignored the bite mark.

I tighten my legs around him, urging him on as I keep on grinding against him, his tongue doing marvels to my flesh. He takes turns between both breasts, sucking, teasing and licking.

"I could feast on you forever," he speaks, his hot breath making me gasp. Taking one bud between his teeth, he bites. Hard.

"Az," I half-moan half yell as I feel a shot of lightning go straight to my core. "I'm so close," I barely manage to words out, but he seems to know exactly what I need as he continues to lavish the same type of attention to the other nipple until I'm spasming in his arms. The cold of the water is promptly forgotten as I feel tingles spread through my entire body."

He grabs me by the ankles, dragging me to him, his hands roaming up my calves.

I follow his movements closely, and just when I think I have his trajectory figured out, he surprises me by grabbing on to my dress with both hands and ripping it in the middle. The dress falls away immediately.

"What are you doing now?"

"The moment you touch me, love, I combust," he drawls, his fingers still drawing circles over my naked flesh. "I'm barely in control as it is. The moment my cock is out, or your god forbid, your hands on it, I'll lose whatever control I have left," his voice is thick and strained, and I can see he's trying to fight himself.

He trails the back of his hand over my damp panties, and my breath catches in my throat as he skims that extremely sensitive part of myself.

"I want to tear you apart and put you back together," he trails his tongue down my face and on my chin, goosebumps appearing all over my skin. "But while I put you back, I'd keep something of yours," his teeth scrape along the curve of my neck, "so that you're never whole without me."

"Yes." I find myself agreeing, even though his words should make me run. "Please," I whisper, and his mouth opens wide right at the junction of my neck, his teeth lodging into my skin and breaking the surface.

Chapter 20

I swear I felt cool liquid dripping down my neck, but When I touched my neck, there was nothing. Az still kept licking the 'mark' that he made. I grew tired of his games and I tugged off the blindfold. My eyes adjust to the lighting and I saw Kael sitting in front of me, naked. His cock was upright, he was watching us.

"Don't stop on my account sweetheart." He said stroking his dick.

He turned towards Auzrael whose eyes were filled with hunger and lust.

"I told you to not touch the blindfold until I told you so." Auzrael said, pinching my right cheek. I moaned at the contact of his rough fingers. I arched my back trying to feel him over me.

"Our little human now has three punishments to her list." Kael said getting up from the couch and bring his cock near my mouth.

He grabbed my face and lifted it up so I could meet his eyes, "Don't cum, or we'll stop everything and you won't have any of us to fill your dripping, warm cunt." He said as he thrusted his hips without a warning.

I opened my mouth wider, moving forward to give a few experimental laps around the crown which is flushed red and stretched tight. His skin is smooth under my tongue, like silk. I can feel the heat of him against my tongue and the slight hint of salt from his skin hits my taste buds. There is light smell of him here, but it is muskier and undecidedly male. I swirl my tongue around a few more times before leaning forward further and replacing my tongue with my lips. He grabs my hair.

I freeze, afraid I did something wrong.

My eyes swing upward while my mouth is still full of his dick. I hum around the turgid length when I see how much he is enjoying my little performance. His excitement is stamped on the features of his face; eyes shining with something other than cruelty, hooded and slumberous with lust. His cheeks are flushed, lips parted to allow the heavy breaths to pass through, and there is a fine sheen of sweat on his brow. His hair messy and perfectly elegant, and I would give anything to feel the cool and silky strands against my skin. Wishful thinking though. It really isn't fair how attractive - no, that's not the right word - sinfully hot, the guy is.

He adjusts his grip on my head and gives a quick thrust into my mouth. The pleasure of the act tightens his features, giving him a savage quality. He does it again, almost hitting the back of my throat, but not quite. Seeming satisfied that I can handle him, he starts pumping into my mouth with more of his length. My gag reflex is indeed triggered, and I can feel my throat convulse around him. He groans and closes his eyes, his expression rapturous. He thrusts a few more times and I can't stop the way my throat wants to stop his invasion, or the tears that are streaming from my eyes. I don't want to miss a single expression or emotion on his face, while he cums into my mouth.

He removes himself from my mouth, I swallow his cum. Kael groans in approval. From behind Az leans in, rubbing his cock over my ass. He licks my ear from behind, just as I was about to lean into his embrace he flips me onto my back and snuggles beside me, "Go to sleep, El." He says.

"I thought-" As I was talking I get cut off my Kael who is now devouring my mouth.

"I can't get enough of you." He moans into my mouth and goes back to playing with my nipples.

"We're sorry, El." Az whispers to me and holds me tight as though I'm going to disappear any moment.

I wanted to ask why he was sorry, as I was going to suddenly everything turns dark.

As the darkness enveloped me, confusion and fear gripped my heart. I reached out instinctively, searching for any semblance of reality, but the void around me was impenetrable. A swirl of emotions churned within, and I desperately tried to grasp onto something, anything, to anchor myself.

Closing my eyes seemed to intensify the darkness, and for a brief, terrifying moment, I felt as though I had been severed from all existence. Time itself felt warped, stretching and compressing in a disorienting dance.

And then, as suddenly as it had begun, the darkness receded. I hesitantly opened my eyes, my surroundings coming into focus once more. My heart raced, my chest heaving as I tried to make sense of what had just transpired.

I found myself in my bed, in the familiar comfort of my room. The soft glow of candlelight cast a warm ambiance, and the scent of familiar herbs hung in the air. The room seemed unchanged, as if I had never left.

Questions still gnawed at the edges of my mind. Had it all been a dream? A vision? Or had I truly been transported to another place, only to return in the blink of an eye?

I rushed to the bathroom, my heart still racing from the disorienting experience. The cool tiles under my feet provided a grounding sensation, a reminder that I was back in the real world. My fingers trembled as I reached for the mirror, anticipation and anxiety mingling within me.

With a deep breath, I faced the mirror, my eyes scanning my reflection for any signs of the marks that Az and Kael had left on me. My gaze fell on my wrists, searching for the delicate imprints that had once adorned my skin.

To my surprise, there was nothing there. No fading traces of their touch, no remnants of the intricate patterns that had been woven into my flesh. It was as if they had never existed, as if the marks had been erased along with the darkness that had enveloped me.

Relief washed over me, mingling with a curious sense of wonder. How could something that had felt so tangible and real just moments ago now be completely gone? The uncertainty gnawed at me, but in that moment, all I could do was accept the inexplicable nature of what had occurred.

As I continued to examine myself in the mirror, my fingers brushed against my skin, a reminder of the very real sensations I had experienced during that otherworldly encounter. The memory of

Az's touch, Kael's presence, and the whispered apologies lingered, etched into my mind even though they had left no visible mark.

With a sigh, I turned away from the mirror, my thoughts a jumble of emotions and questions. The events of the day had left me with more mysteries than answers, and I knew that if I wanted to make sense of it all.

I left the bathroom and crossed the room to my desk, where my notebook lay open. I picked up the pen, its weight reassuring in my hand, and began to write. My thoughts poured onto the page, a record of my experiences, my emotions, and my resolve to uncover the truth that lay hidden beneath the surface.

Lost in my thoughts, the scratching of the pen against the paper offered a rhythmic comfort. Each stroke of the pen felt like a step closer to untangling the web of mysteries that surrounded me. The words flowed, forming a testament to my determination to seek the truth, to uncover the secrets that had been hidden from me.

Just as I was engrossed in my writing, the soft voice of Sofia, my fellow attendant, broke through my concentration. "Elvira, we have to gather for a meeting. Behomath has ordered it."

I glanced up from my notebook, meeting Sofia's gaze. Her expression held a mix of seriousness and worry, a reflection of the weight that the demon's orders carried.

"Another meeting?" I asked, my tone tinged with curiosity and apprehension. The summoning of the attendants for a meeting wasn't unusual, but the urgency in Sofia's voice hinted that there was more to this one.

Sofia nodded, her eyes flickering with a mix of emotions. "Yes, it seems important. You know how it goes—when Behomath calls, we must attend."

I sighed, closing my notebook and setting the pen aside. The mysteries of my own experiences would have to wait as duty called. Rising from my desk, I followed Sofia out of the room and into the grand hall where the meeting was to take place.

The hall was vast, its ornate architecture a stark contrast to the apprehension that seemed to hang in the air. Attendees from various corners of the demon kingdom had gathered, their expressions a mixture of tension and submission. It was well known that defying a high ranking's summons was not an option.

Behomath, the imposing demon official, stood at the head of the hall. His presence commanded respect, and his dark eyes swept over the assembled attendants. The room was hushed, a silence borne out of reverence and perhaps a hint of fear.

Behomath's gaze settled on a group of girls clustered together, their heads lowered. They seemed almost afraid to lift their eyes, their posture reflecting a submission that was unsettling. A sense of unease settled within me as I realized that something unusual was afoot.

As the meeting began, Behomath's deep voice resonated throughout the hall. His words were measured, his tone carrying an air of authority that left no room for doubt. My attention was drawn to the group of girls he had singled out. Whispers floated through the air, carried by the attendants around me.

"They're the ones," one girl murmured.

"The chosen ones," another added.

I strained to catch more of their conversation, my curiosity piqued. And then, the words that reached my ears turned my unease into something far darker.

"They're the girls sent to sleep with Kael," someone whispered.

My heart clenched at the realization, my eyes widening in shock. The room seemed to close in around me as I listened to the murmurs. The tension in the hall became suffocating as I tried to overhear more details.

And then, as if the weight of the revelations wasn't enough, a hushed conversation reached my ears—one that sent a shiver down my spine.

"Kael is a monster in bed," a voice said, filled with a mixture of fear and awe. "Many girls couldn't handle him. They say some have even... died."

My heart raced, and a chill ran down my spine. The image of Kael, the demon prince, transformed from a figure of authority to something far more ominous. The complexities of the demon kingdom, the truths that had remained hidden, were slowly unraveling before me, revealing a world of darkness and danger that I had only glimpsed from the periphery.

As the conversation continued around me, my mind was consumed by the disturbing revelations about Kael, the enigmatic demon prince. The hushed whispers painted a picture of him as a force of nature, a figure who inspired both fear and awe. The mention of girls who had suffered, even perished, in his company added a chilling layer to the narrative.

And then, amidst the tension and unease, a voice spoke up, breaking through the hushed discussions. "I don't mind," a girl's voice rang out, her tone oddly defiant. "If it's Kael, I'll gladly lay my pussy out for him."

The words hung in the air like a heavy silence, their impact sending a shiver down my spine. I turned to see the girl who had spoken, her eyes filled with a strange determination. She seemed resolute, unafraid of the stories that had circulated about Kael's encounters.

But for me, those words were like a sharp knife twisting in my gut. A mixture of jealousy and anger surged within me, catching me off guard.

The unease settled deep within me, gnawing at my thoughts. It wasn't just the fear that this girl's decision represented; it was the anger that someone would touch my kael. My kael? What am I saying?

Sofia, who stood beside me, seemed to sense my inner turmoil. Her gaze met mine, and her expression held a mixture of sympathy and understanding. She knew that the revelations were a lot to process, that the darkness of this world was a heavy burden to bear.

But despite Sofia's silent support, I felt a storm of emotions swirling within me—jealousy over this girl's confidence, anger at her recklessness, and a profound sense of unease at the thought of Kael's touch on someone else.

As the attendees began to disperse, my gaze remained fixed on the girl who had spoken so defiantly. Her determination was both puzzling and concerning. What kind of circumstances could lead someone to willingly face the dangers that lurked in the shadows, to embrace the unknown with such recklessness?

Lost in thought, I turned to leave the grand hall, intent on seeking solace in the solitude of my quarters. But just as I was about to step away, a firm hand clamped onto my arm, halting my movement abruptly. My heart raced as I turned to face Behomath.

"Elvira," his voice was low and resonant, a tone that brooked no argument. "Walk with me."

His command was clear, and I found myself unable to refuse. I followed him as he led the way, my unease growing with each step. The corridors we traversed were dimly lit, the atmosphere heavy with an unsettling tension.

Eventually, Behomath halted in front of a set of massive, ornate doors. The sight of them sent a chill down my spine, and a sense of foreboding settled over me. The dungeons—rumored to be a place of punishment and darkness.

The doors creaked open, revealing a dimly lit chamber beyond. Behomath's grip on my arm tightened as he guided me inside, and my heart raced as I took in the scene before me.

Kael stood in the center of the chamber, his presence commanding and enigmatic. His dark eyes held a depth that seemed to penetrate the very core of my being, and the intensity of his gaze left me feeling exposed and vulnerable.

I felt a mixture of fear and curiosity, my gaze locked onto Kael's form. The air in the room seemed to crackle with tension, and the weight of his presence pressed down upon me like an invisible force.

"Elvira," Behomath's voice interrupted my thoughts, drawing my attention back to him. "I've brought her, your highness."

I shifted my gaze to Kael from Behomath, a sense of trepidation settling within me. Kael's presence radiated an aura of enigma and danger that left me on edge. His dark eyes met mine, and for a moment, it felt as though the room had fallen into an eerie silence.

Kael's lips curled into a sinister smile, a gesture that sent a shiver down my spine. The dim light of the dungeon played upon his features, casting shadows that seemed to dance around him. In that moment, he seemed both alluring and dangerous, a dichotomy that made my heart race.

But it wasn't just his presence that caught my attention—it was the state he was in. The blood that marred his clothes and stained his hands created a stark contrast to his pale skin. The sight of it was jarring, sending a wave of unease through me. As my gaze lingered on the blood, questions tumbled through my mind. What had happened? What had he been involved in? The darkness that surrounded Kael seemed to take on a tangible form, a cloak of secrecy and violence that sent a chill down my spine.

As the silence hung heavy in the air, Kael's lips curled into a wicked smile that seemed to reflect the very shadows that enveloped him. His dark eyes held mine, an intensity that was both disconcerting and captivating. Without breaking his gaze, he lifted his blood-stained fingers to his lips and casually licked the crimson fluid.

The sight was unnerving, sending a shiver down my spine. It was as if he reveled in the violence and darkness that surrounded him, as if he were a part of it. The unease within me deepened, and I took a hesitant step back, my heart racing as his presence seemed to close in around me.

"Elvira," his voice was a low murmur, the timbre sending a jolt through me. "Do you fear me?"

His words hung in the air, a challenge that carried an underlying threat. The question was laced with a darkness that I couldn't quite decipher. Fear, curiosity, and a stubborn defiance warred within me. I refused to let his aura intimidate me, to let the enigma of his being overwhelm my senses.

"I fear what I do not understand," I replied, my voice steady despite the turmoil within me. "And there is much about you that remains a mystery, yet there's a small part that does not fear you."

Kael's smile widened, his movements fluid as he took a deliberate step closer. His presence seemed to fill the room, his aura an intoxicating blend of danger and allure. My heart raced as his gaze bore into mine, a challenge that dared me to look beyond the surface, to uncover the truths that were veiled in darkness.

The tension in the room was palpable, a dance of power and vulnerability. I was caught in his orbit, drawn to the enigmatic energy that surrounded him even as my instincts urged me to be cautious.

"Ah, Elvira," he murmured, his voice a velvety whisper. "Mysteries are what keep life interesting, don't you think?"

His words held a certain seductive quality, a tantalizing suggestion that pulled at something deep within me. My gaze flickered to the blood that still stained his fingers, a stark reminder of the darkness that lingered beneath his exterior.

As he closed the distance between us, his proximity sending a rush of conflicting emotions through me, I couldn't deny the magnetic pull he had over me. The air seemed charged with a primal energy, an attraction that defied reason.

His words held a certain seductive quality, a tantalizing suggestion that pulled at something deep within me. My gaze flickered to the blood that still stained his fingers, a stark reminder of the darkness that lingered beneath his exterior.

For a moment, the charged atmosphere seemed to envelop us, the tension between us almost palpable. My heart raced, and an unexpected heat spread through my veins. It was an intoxicating mixture of fear and arousal, a clash of emotions that both intrigued and disturbed me.

As Kael's gaze held mine, his dark eyes seemed to see right through me, igniting a spark that I couldn't ignore.

My lips parted as if to respond, but no words came forth. The charged silence seemed to stretch between us, a battle of wills and desires that played out in the unspoken space.

As Kael's gaze held mine, his dark eyes seemed to see right through me, igniting a spark that I couldn't ignore. The intensity of his stare sent a rush of heat through me, a mix of both apprehension and an inexplicable attraction that I struggled to reconcile.

Suddenly, Kael's lips curved into a knowing smile, his expression one of amusement and something deeper—something that sent a fresh wave of heat through me. His gaze shifted from my eyes to my slightly parted lips, and I felt a jolt of both vulnerability and anticipation.

With deliberate slowness, Kael lifted one of his blood-stained fingers and traced it along my bottom lip. The touch was feather-light, almost a caress, yet the blood that marked his finger created a startling contrast against my skin.

A gasp caught in my throat, a mixture of surprise and an unexpected rush of desire. The intimacy of the gesture, the sensation of his touch against my lips, sent my heart into a frenzied rhythm.

Kael's smile deepened, his eyes never leaving mine as he continued to trace the curve of my lip. It was as if he could sense the turmoil within me, the conflicting emotions that roiled beneath the surface.

"You're quite the mystery, Elvira," he murmured, his voice a low timbre that seemed to resonate within me. "There's a fire in your eyes, a tension in your stance."

His words were both an observation and a tease, a reminder of the arousal that simmered just beneath the surface. My cheeks flushed with a mixture of embarrassment and a renewed surge of desire.

I tried to find my voice, to respond to his words, but the intensity of the moment left me feeling unsteady. It was as though he held a power over me, a power that I couldn't quite escape, no matter how much I tried to resist.

As Kael's finger left my lips, the absence of his touch left a lingering ache. The charged atmosphere remained, the unspoken tension a reminder of the uncharted territory that lay before us. My heart raced, my senses heightened by the intimacy of the moment and the enigmatic pull he held over me.

Suddenly, Kael's expression shifted, his lips curling into a sinister smile that sent a fresh wave of unease through me. The shift in his demeanor was palpable, a reminder of the darkness that lurked beneath the surface. Without a word, he turned and began to walk, expecting me to follow.

The dungeon's cold and damp atmosphere seemed to close in around us as I stepped into the dimly lit corridor. The flickering torches cast eerie shadows on the stone walls, the very air heavy with the weight of secrets and darkness.

Kael's strides were purposeful, leading me deeper into the labyrinthine passages. I followed, my heart pounding, the unease in the pit of my stomach growing with each step. The dungeon was a place of punishment and confinement, a realm of nightmares that I had never imagined finding myself in.

My mind raced with questions, with a mounting sense of dread. What did Kael intend to show me? What darkness awaited us in these shadowy depths?

Finally, he stopped before a heavy, iron-clad door. The air seemed to grow colder, a shiver running down my spine as I took in the ominous sight before me. Without a word, Kael pushed the door open, revealing a small, dimly lit cell within.

My heart sank as I realized the gravity of the situation. The cell was a bleak, desolate space—a stark contrast to the opulence of the demon kingdom I had seen thus far. The walls seemed to close in around me, the very atmosphere filled with a sense of foreboding.

Kael's gaze met mine, and there was a purposeful glint in his eyes. He gestured for me to step inside, his expression unreadable. The shadows seemed to dance around him, his presence an enigma that both fascinated and terrified me.

The weight of the moment settled upon my shoulders as I stepped into the cell, the door closing behind me with a heavy thud. I felt a rush of panic, a sensation of being trapped both physically and emotionally.

As I turned to face Kael, my lips parted to form a question, but the words remained unspoken. The tension between us was palpable, the truth of our situation undeniable. I was alone in the depths of the dungeon with the enigmatic demon prince, a darkness looming over us that I couldn't quite grasp.

Chapter 22

As I turned to face Kael, my lips parted to form a question, but the words remained unspoken. The tension between us was palpable, the truth of our situation undeniable. I was alone in the depths of the dungeon with the demon prince, a darkness looming over us that I couldn't quite grasp.

My gaze shifted beyond Kael, taking in the dimly lit cell. But what caught my attention was the sight that greeted me-an image of horror that sent a jolt of shock through my veins.

There, chained to the wall, was a man who seemed to hover on the edge of death. His face was bloodied and bruised, his body showing signs of brutal mistreatment. My heart clenched at the sight of him, the reality of the cruelty that existed within these dungeon walls hitting me with a visceral force.

Around the man lay several lifeless bodies, the air heavy with the metallic scent of blood. The scene was one of carnage and despair, a stark reminder of the darkness that engulfed this place. The blood pooled around the bodies, staining the cold stone floor with a chilling reminder of the violence that had taken place.

I stared in shock, my breath catching in my throat. The realization of the brutality that had unfolded in this cell was a harsh reality that I couldn't ignore. The man's tortured form, the dead bodies that surrounded him-it was a tableau of horror that spoke of pain and suffering beyond measure.

Kael's presence beside me felt even more ominous in the wake of the gruesome scene. I turned to him, a mix of anger and sadness swirling within me. The questions burned in my mind, demanding answers that I feared might reveal even darker truths.

"Why have you brought me here, Kael?" My voice quivered with a mixture of emotions-disbelief, horror, and a determination to uncover the truth. "What is this place? What has happened here?"

The silence stretched between us, a heavy tension that seemed to amplify the gruesome scene before me. My gaze remained locked on Kael, seeking answers, seeking a way to make sense of the nightmare that unfolded within the cell.

And then, Kael's voice broke through the stillness, a mocking softness that sent a shiver down my spine. It was as if he were speaking to a child, a tone that belied the darkness of the scene before us.

"Do you not like it?" he asked, his words dripping with a sinister amusement. His gaze remained fixed on me, his eyes holding a challenge that dared me to comprehend the depths of his intent.

The question was absurd, the situation beyond my understanding. The man chained to the wall, the lifeless bodies strewn around him-the horror of it all was undeniable. The implication that I might "like" it was both infuriating and chilling.

My anger flared, and I met Kael's gaze with a mixture of incredulity and defiance. "This... this is beyond any semblance of humanity, Kael. How can you stand here and mock such suffering?"

As my words filled the air, the weight of the situation bore down on me with a renewed force. Kael's demeanor, the callousness of his tone, hinted at a darkness that was beyond my comprehension. It was as if he reveled in the chaos and violence that surrounded us, as if he was testing the limits of my understanding and resolve.

And then, Kael's lips curved into a mocking smile, his amusement seemingly unending. "Humanity?" he repeated, his voice dripping with cynicism. "Elvira, you seem to forget that I am not bound by the frail notions of humanity. I am a demon, after all."

The reminder was chilling, a stark contrast to the way I had tried to view the demon kingdom. My quest for understanding, for compassion, was met with a reality that was far more sinister and twisted.

As if to emphasize his point, Kael's gaze shifted from mine to a blade that lay nearby. He picked it up with casual grace, the glint of metal catching the dim light of the cell. My breath caught as the implications of his actions settled upon me-this was a place of torture, a chamber of horrors that defied reason.

"I exist beyond the morality and constraints of your world," he continued, his tone almost conversational. "This is a realm of darkness, Elvira, and you would do well to remember that."

The blade in his hand gleamed, its edges sharp and deadly. The implication was clear, and a wave of apprehension washed over me. I was standing on the precipice of something far more dangerous than I had ever imagined, facing a being who was the embodiment of a darkness that I couldn't comprehend.

In that moment, I couldn't deny the fear that churned within me. The demon prince before me was an enigma, a force of both attraction and repulsion. The darkness that he exuded was intoxicating and terrifying all at once, a duality that left me struggling to navigate the depths of his intentions.

"Kael," I began, my voice barely above a whisper, "were any of it ... true? Or were they merely part of some twisted game?"

My words hung in the air, the weight of uncertainty and vulnerability accompanying them. The memories of our interactions, the moments that had seemed intimate and tender, now seemed clouded by the darkness that surrounded us. I wanted to believe that there had been a glimmer of sincerity between us, that not everything was a facade. But in the face of the horrors that I had witnessed, doubt gnawed at me, a relentless companion in this realm of uncertainty.

Kael's gaze held mine, his eyes unreadable. For a moment, the air seemed to still, the tension between us almost tangible.

But instead of answering, Kael's attention shifted, as if he were deliberately avoiding the question that had been poised. His demeanor shifted, his focus turning toward the man chained to the wall-the man who had been subjected to unimaginable suffering.

My breath caught as I watched Kael's actions unfold before me. He advanced toward the bloodied and battered figure, his steps deliberate, the blade he held glinting ominously in the dim light. The man's pained and pleading gaze met mine briefly, his eyes a desperate plea for mercy.

"Please," the man's voice was a hoarse whisper, a plea for his life that echoed in the confines of the cell. "I beg you... have mercy."

But Kael's response was cold and unyielding. He turned a deaf ear to the man's cries, his actions devoid of empathy as he raised the blade, his intent clear. The horror of the situation was overwhelming, a chilling reminder of the darkness that resided within the demon prince.

"Stop!" My voice trembled with a mix of fear and desperation as I stepped forward, my heart pounding in my chest. The sight before me was a nightmare, a stark portrayal of cruelty that I couldn't comprehend. "Please, Kael, you must stop this!"

My plea fell on deaf ears, Kael's focus unwavering as he continued his approach. The man's pleas grew more desperate, the fear in his eyes reflecting the agony he was enduring. The blade in Kael's hand seemed to symbolize not only the imminent danger to the man but also the darkness that permeated this realm.

As Kael raised the blade, my voice cracked with a mixture of anguish and desperation. "I beg you, Kael, this is not you. Show mercy. Show that there's more to you than this."

For a heartbeat that felt like an eternity, the air was heavy with the tension of the moment. I watched, my heart in my throat, as Kael held the blade aloft, the man's pleas echoing in the air like a haunting refrain. And then, as if suspended in time, Kael's actions abruptly ceased, the blade freezing in its trajectory.

His gaze met mine, his eyes filled with a chilling amusement that sent shivers down my spine. His lips curled into a mocking smile, the weight of his gaze a reminder of the power he held over me, over this entire macabre scene.

"You think you know me, Elvira?" His voice was a mixture of mockery and something darker, something that sent a fresh wave of apprehension through me. "You believe that your glimpses into my world have shown you the truth? You know nothing of what I am, of what I'm capable of."

The truth of his words hit me like a blow, a reminder of the complexities that lay beneath the surface. My heart ached as I stood there, tears welling in my eyes, the man's cries for mercy still ringing in my ears.

"You're right," I admitted, my voice trembling with a mixture of defeat and sorrow. "I don't fully understand, but what I do know is that there's a part of you that's been buried beneath this darkness. A part that I've seen glimpses of, however fleeting they may be."

Kael's laughter cut through the air, a chilling sound that seemed to reverberate within the cell. "Fleeting? You're a naive fool, Elvira. Your beliefs are as fragile as the humans you so desperately try to understand."

Tears trickled down my cheeks, my heart heavy with a combination of helplessness and a determination to uncover the truth. The man's fate remained uncertain, the darkness that Kael exuded was a weight that seemed to press down on me, suffocating any semblance of hope.

With a trembling voice, I took a step closer to Kael, my desperation outweighing my fear. "Please, Kael," I implored, my voice catching in my throat. "Let me take his place. Do whatever you wish with me instead. Spare him."

The man's cries for mercy echoed in my ears, a haunting backdrop to my plea. I looked into Kael's eyes, my gaze unwavering, fueled by a mixture of compassion and a desperate need to prevent further suffering. My heart ached for the man, a stranger caught in the clutches of this horrifying reality.

Kael's gaze held mine, his expression inscrutable as he considered my words. For a moment, the air seemed to thicken, the tension between us almost tangible. The weight of his decision hung in the balance, the darkness that surrounded him a barrier I couldn't breach.

And then, he laughed-a low, humorless sound that sent a shiver down my spine. "You truly are a remarkable creature, Elvira," he mused, his amusement at my plea evident. "But your willingness to sacrifice yourself for the sake of a stranger... it's almost endearing."

His words were laced with a bitter irony, a reminder of the complexities of his nature. In the midst of this grim situation, Kael's response was a reminder that the lines between cruelty and amusement were blurred in this realm.

The man's agonized cries continued, a stark reminder of the urgency of the situation. But even as I stood there, tears staining my cheeks, I couldn't shake the feeling that my plea had fallen on deaf ears. The darkness that enveloped Kael seemed impenetrable, a force that defied my every attempt to understand or influence.

As the man's pleas reached a fever pitch, I looked at Kael one last time, my voice a desperate whisper. "Please, Kael."

Kael's gaze held mine, his expression unreadable as he seemed to consider my plea. And then, with a calculated glint in his eyes, he spoke in a tone that sent a shiver down my spine.

"I will spare this man," he began, his voice dripping with a sinister amusement, "but only if you agree to do something for me."

My heart pounded in my chest, a mixture of relief and trepidation coursing through me. The man's cries for mercy still echoed in the air, a reminder of the stakes of this grim negotiation. I met Kael's gaze, my voice barely steady as I asked, "What do you want me to do?"

His lips curved into a chilling smile, his eyes dancing with a dangerous gleam. "There's a task that I need someone to complete-a task that requires a certain... finesse and resourcefulness. If you agree to undertake it, I will grant him peace."

The words hung in the air, heavy with implications that sent a chill down my spine. The man's desperate pleas for mercy had shifted to a new urgency as he struggled against his restraints, his voice hoarse with fear. I met Kael's gaze, a mixture of apprehension and resolve settling within me.

And then, as if heeding an inner call, I turned to face the man whose fate was now intertwined with mine. My voice was steady, even as I offered him a reassuring glance. "Don't worry," I said softly, my words carrying a determination that I hoped would reach him. "I'll be fine. Nothing will happen to me."

His wide eyes held a mixture of disbelief and gratitude, his protests silenced by the weight of his helplessness. I wished I could do more, wished that the path I was about to tread didn't involve such dire choices. But the reality before me was stark-the man's life depended on my decision, and I couldn't turn away from the opportunity to save him.

As I turned back to face Kael, his gaze held mine, the challenge and expectation evident. The choice was mine to make, the consequences mine to bear. The darkness that clung to him was a reminder that whatever task he had in mind, it wouldn't be without its share of danger and moral complexity.

But in the depths of that dungeon, where shadows danced and the cries of the suffering lingered, I made my choice.

"I agree."

The words left my lips, carrying with them a weight that settled over the cell like a shroud. The deal was struck, my decision made. The man's desperate pleas had softened into a resigned silence, his eyes now holding a mixture of relief and gratitude.

As Kael stepped closer, his gaze locked onto mine, a chilling sense of finality settled over the cell. The man's fate hung in the balance, and with a sudden, calculated movement, Kael's blade found its mark. The man's agonized cries shattered the air, the metallic tang of blood filling my senses as life ebbed away.

"No!" The cry was torn from my throat, a guttural sound that echoed in the confines of the cell. Horror gripped me as I watched the life drain from the man, the reality of what had just transpired sending shockwaves through my senses.

"You didn't stick to your deal," I gasped, my voice a mixture of horror and accusation. "You said you would spare him if I agreed."

Kael's lips curled into a chilling smile, his eyes devoid of remorse as he wiped the bloodied blade clean. His response was laced with a sinister amusement, a reminder of the darkness that he embodied.

"I said I would grant him peace," he replied, his voice like a cold whisper in the darkness. "And I did. He is free from suffering now."

The implication of his words hit me like a blow, a brutal reminder that the realm of demons operated by its own twisted logic. The man's cries had been silenced, his life taken, but according to Kael's warped perspective, the deal had been upheld.

In that moment, I was left grappling with a sickening mix of horror, anger, and an overwhelming sense of helplessness. The darkness that Kael represented, the choices he forced me to make-it was a reality that defied any semblance of humanity, a realm where cruelty and manipulation held sway.

As Kael turned away, leaving the lifeless form behind, I was left standing in the aftermath of his cruel game.

Chapter 23

As I stood at the sink, the water swirling around the dishes in my hands, my mind couldn't help but drift back to the harrowing incident in the dungeons with Kael. The memory was etched into my thoughts, each detail vivid and unsettling. The way he had held that blade, the calculating glint in his eyes, and the chilling nonchalance with which he had taken a life—it was a tableau of darkness that refused to fade.

My hands moved mechanically, the scrubbing of the dishes a futile attempt to distract myself from the haunting images that replayed in my mind. But even as I focused on the task at hand, my thoughts were consumed by questions that had no easy answers.

Kael's behavior had been odd, even within the context of the demon kingdom's brutality. It was as if he reveled in the darkness, as if the pain and suffering were his playthings. And yet, there had been moments—brief glimmers of something more nuanced, more conflicted. I remembered the times he had allowed vulnerability to surface, the times when his guard had slipped.

It was those moments that confounded me, that left me struggling to reconcile the enigma that was Kael. His actions in the
dungeons were a stark reminder of the darkness that resided within
him, but there were facets to him that defied easy categorization.
It was as if his very nature was a tapestry woven with threads of
cruelty and hints of something deeper, something that eluded my
understanding.

As I continued to scrub the dishes, a mix of unease and determination settled within me. The incident had left a mark on my
perception of the demon kingdom, a mark that I couldn't ignore. I
had glimpsed the darkness that lurked beneath the surface, and it
was a truth that demanded further exploration.

Yet, amid the echoes of that dark encounter, my thoughts also
wandered to the moments of vulnerability I had witnessed in Kael.
The way he had let his guard down, the hints of something deeper
hidden behind the layers of cruelty and intrigue—it was a duality
that perplexed me.

I couldn't forget the fleeting touches, the shared glances, the
moments when the darkness seemed to recede, allowing a glimpse
of something more complex. There had been instances when Kael's
demeanor had shifted, when his gaze had held a certain weight that
hinted at a struggle beneath the surface.

As I scrubbed the dishes mechanically, my mind's eye replayed
those moments. The way his voice had softened, the look in his eyes
that defied the cruelty he was capable of—these were the enigmatic
facets that I couldn't ignore. In the midst of the darkness that
surrounded him, there were shades of something that challenged
my understanding of the demon prince.

But even as I delved into those memories, I couldn't ignore the caution that accompanied them. Kael was an enigma, a figure whose complexity I had yet to unravel fully. The darkness he exuded was a formidable force, a force that threatened to consume everything in its path.

As I rinsed the last dish and placed it on the drying rack, my thoughts remained a whirlwind of conflicting emotions.

The incident had left a mark on my perception of the demon kingdom, a mark that I couldn't ignore. I had glimpsed the darkness that lurked beneath the surface, and it was a truth that demanded further exploration.

The routine sounds of the castle were interrupted by the arrival of Behomath, the Royal demon courtier, his presence announced by the echoing footsteps that reverberated through the halls. I glanced towards the entrance, my hands stilling in their task, as he entered the room. His presence carried an air of authority, and as his gaze locked onto mine, a chill seemed to settle in the air.

"Elvira," his voice was a low, drawling sound that seemed to hold a mixture of annoyance and amusement. "You are summoned at the court."

I wiped my hands on a nearby cloth, a feeling of trepidation settling within me. The demon court was a realm of politics and power plays, a place where my presence was both a curiosity and an oddity. As I followed Behomath through the halls of the castle, his words cut through the air like a blade.

"You know, Elvira," he said, his tone dripping with a mocking familiarity, "you're quite the nuisance here, aren't you? Always creating problems, stirring the pot."

I walked alongside him, my gaze fixed ahead as I navigated the maze-like corridors. His words were a reminder of the delicate balance I held in this realm—a balance between the curiosity that drove me to uncover the truth and the danger that lurked in the shadows.

"I don't intend to cause trouble," I replied, my voice steady despite the unease that simmered beneath the surface.

Behomath's laughter was a dark, hollow sound that seemed to echo down the corridor. "Oh, you're quite the idealist, Elvira. You think you can change things here? Just because you have both the princes 'fancy-ing' you, makes you powerful? Just wait until they get bored of a human, a species who cannot handle their adrenaline and sex drive."

His words held a cynical edge, a reminder that the demon kingdom was a place of complexities far beyond my understanding. Yet, even in the face of his mockery, a fire burned within me—a fire that refused to be extinguished by the cynicism that surrounded me.

"I'm not seeking power," I retorted, my voice tinged with frustration.

Behomath's gaze turned cold, a dangerous glint in his eyes. "You're a human, Elvira. Your very existence here is a curiosity, a fleeting amusement for beings who thrive on chaos and dominance. Don't delude yourself into thinking you're anything more."

His words were a sharp reminder of the divide that existed between our worlds, the barriers that couldn't be ignored. Before I could respond, Behomath raised a hand to silence me, his expression growing colder.

"Enough," he snapped, his voice cutting through the air like a blade. "Your naivety is astounding. You're here because the princes find you intriguing, because they seek to amuse themselves with your presence. But don't mistake their fleeting interest for anything more. The demon court is not a place for sentimentality or foolish dreams."

I was taken aback by the intensity of his words, the weight of his cynicism crashing over me like a tidal wave. The fire that had burned within me moments ago now felt like a flicker against the overwhelming darkness that he portrayed.

As Behomath turned and continued down the corridor, leaving me with his biting words, I was left grappling with a mix of emotions. The demon kingdom's complexities, the harsh realities that defined it, were a force that couldn't be dismissed. And yet, deep within me, that fire of determination still smoldered—a fire that refused to let the darkness swallow me whole, a fire that would drive me to uncover the truths that lay beyond the shadows.

As I stepped into the demon court, a hush seemed to settle over the grand chamber. The air was heavy with an aura of power and intrigue, the very essence of the demon kingdom palpable in every corner. The walls were adorned with intricate tapestries depicting scenes of conquest and dominance, each thread woven with a history that spanned countless generations.

The chamber was vast, its architecture a blend of opulence and intimidation. Enormous pillars stretched towards the vaulted ceiling, their surfaces etched with symbols and runes that glowed with an otherworldly energy. Torches lined the walls, casting flickering shadows that danced in harmony with the murmurs of the assembled courtiers.

At the heart of the chamber, seated upon a grand, obsidian throne, was the figure of ultimate authority—the demon king. His presence exuded power, his form cloaked in regal attire that matched the darkness of his realm. His eyes, intense and calculating, swept across the court as if assessing each individual with a scrutiny that sent shivers down the spines of those present.

And to the king's right, sat the embodiment of the darkness I had witnessed in the dungeons—Prince Kael. His presence was magnetic, his aura one of danger and intrigue. Unlike Auzrael's composed posture, Kael's lean form seemed to exude an unsettling energy, his dark eyes holding a mix of curiosity and challenge as they scanned the court.

And to the king's left sat Prince Auzrael, an embodiment of dominion and authority. His form was a study in regal elegance, every movement calculated and controlled. An emotionless mask concealed his features, his eyes veiled behind a façade that gave away nothing. What hurt me was, Princess Isabel sitting in his lap. Her fingers traced a delicate pattern on Auzrael's arm as she leaned into his side, a silent display of her allegiance.

The dynamics of the court were laid bare before me—the intricate dance of power, allegiance, and intrigue that defined this realm. As I stood on the periphery, an outsider in this web of politics and manipulation, I couldn't help but feel a mix of awe and trepidation.

Prince Kael's gaze, filled with curiosity and challenge, remained fixed on the courtiers. His presence seemed to draw them in, a magnetic force that held their attention even in the midst of the king's imposing aura. It was as if his very being commanded their curiosity, a reflection of the enigma that surrounded him.

As I stood at the entrance, my presence a stark contrast to the court's denizens, I couldn't shake the feeling that every eye was upon me. The demon court was a realm of power plays and hidden agendas, a place where appearances could be deceiving and loyalties were ever-shifting. It was a world of darkness and intrigue, and as I prepared to navigate its complexities, I knew that the truths I sought would come at a price.

The king's gaze, intense and penetrating, settled on me as if dissecting every facet of my being. His words, delivered with a calculated tone, reverberated through the chamber like a somber echo. "This is it?"

Though his statement was seemingly innocuous, there was an undercurrent of scrutiny that left me feeling exposed, as if my very presence had been placed under a magnifying glass. The weight of his gaze seemed to assess not only my physical appearance but also the significance of my existence within the demon court.

For a fleeting moment, I felt a surge of vulnerability—standing before the figure of ultimate authority, a human amidst beings whose motives and intentions were shrouded in layers of complexity. The king's words were a reminder that I was an outsider in this realm, an anomaly whose purpose was both a curiosity and a potential threat.

As I held the weight of his gaze, I couldn't ignore the unease that settled within me. The demon court was a place where power dynamics were in constant flux, and the king's inscrutable expression hinted at a depth of understanding that far surpassed my own.

As I held the weight of the king's gaze, my vulnerability was like an exposed nerve. The court's complexity and the enigma of its inhabitants felt almost overwhelming. I couldn't shake the feeling of being an interloper in a realm where every step held hidden consequences.

Amidst this tumultuous sea of thoughts, Prince Kael's voice cut through the air—a reminder that I was not alone in my unease.

"She won't last long here," Kael's voice was laced with a dark amusement, his eyes meeting mine with a challenge that sent shivers down my spine. "It's only a matter of time before she's broken. Her human spirit is fragile, and my demon... well, he's quite eager to see her spirit shattered."

His words were a jarring contrast to the glimmers of vulnerability I had seen in him before. It was as if he reveled in the idea of chaos, his dark side seeking to exploit my very presence in this place of darkness and intrigue.

As Kael's gaze held mine, a sense of defiance rose within me. While I couldn't deny the challenges that lay ahead, I was determined to prove him wrong—to show that my purpose here wasn't as fragile as he believed. The demon prince's words were a call to arms, igniting a determination that burned brighter in the face of adversity.

But as I held Kael's gaze, I couldn't help but wonder about the complexity that defined him. The darkness and the intrigue he exuded were inextricably woven into his identity. And even as I resisted the shadow he cast over me.

Before I could respond to Kael's taunts, a new voice sliced through the tension-laden air—the chilling resonance of Prince Auzrael's words.

"She's my toy," Auzrael's tone was possessive, and his gaze bore into me with a mixture of entitlement and detachment. "And I don't appreciate my toys being damaged."

His words hung in the air, a stark reminder of the dynamic between us. Yet, before I could process his declaration, the king's voice cut through the room with an authority that sent a shiver down my spine.

"Worthless," the king's voice was dismissive, as if casting judgment upon me from his throne. "She's hardly something fit for a prince of your stature, Auzrael. Your time would be better spent elsewhere."

The king's words were like a cold blade, a reminder that in this realm, I was a pawn in a game of power that I could scarcely comprehend. The sense of worthlessness washed over me, a chilling realization of my place in this court's hierarchy.

Yet, amidst the weight of the king's judgment, my gaze flickered towards Prince Kael. The stiffness in his posture was a subtle indication of a reaction he couldn't quite conceal. His eyes held a glint of something—anger, defiance, or perhaps something deeper that I couldn't decipher.

As the king's words indirectly insinuated that Kael wasn't worth the finery and attention given to Auzrael, a whirlwind of emotions stirred within me. The complexities of the court, the motives of its inhabitants, seemed to shift and twist in a dance of power and ambition.

As the tense atmosphere in the court lingered, the king's attention shifted towards Prince Kael—a figure who exuded an air of both danger and defiance.

"Kael," the king's voice carried a tone of calculated authority, "you are granted the privilege of going through these efforts for a purpose. Your demon's nature is unruly, and the Blood Moon night approaches. We cannot afford any disruptions."

The significance of the king's words hung in the air, a reminder that beneath the surface of this realm lay a reality defined by forces far beyond my understanding. The mention of the Blood Moon night held an air of foreboding, a sense that the darkness I had glimpsed was only a fraction of the complexity that would unfold.

As Kael's gaze met the king's, a tension seemed to crackle between them. The layers of unspoken motives, allegiances, and responsibilities played out in this moment of revelation. The king's authority was a reminder that even the enigmatic prince, with all his defiance, was subject to the rules and dynamics of the demon kingdom—a realm where power was wielded with a precision that left no room for sentimentality.

"Why not just exile me then, if I'm such a trouble?" Kael's words dripped with a bitterness that underscored the depth of his frustration. His eyes, intense and unyielding, locked onto the king's gaze, holding a level of audacity that seemed to challenge the very foundations of the realm's power dynamics.

The court seemed to hold its breath, the unspoken tension between prince and king palpable. The complexity of their dynamic was laid bare—an enigmatic prince pushing back against the authority that sought to rein him in, a king asserting his dominion with a firmness that brooked no dissent.

In the charged silence that followed Kael's biting words, the king's response was a calculated stroke—a retort that cut to the core of the enigmatic prince's defiance.

"Exile you?" The king's voice held a mix of condescension and offense, his gaze unwavering as it locked onto Kael's. "You forget your place, Kael. You're here not by chance, but because you serve a purpose. You're a formidable asset in times of war, a strong demon that can be harnessed."

The weight of the king's words seemed to hang in the air, an unspoken reminder of the role Kael played within the grand tapestry of the demon kingdom's machinations. The tension that crackled between prince and king was a testament to the intricacies that governed this court—a realm where power was synonymous with survival, and loyalty was a commodity that held the threads of fate in its grasp.

As I watched this exchange, I couldn't help but sense the undercurrents of vulnerability that ran beneath their bravado. The king's authority was rooted in pragmatism, a reminder that even the most enigmatic figures were bound by the roles they fulfilled. And Kael's defiance, while audacious, was a reflection of his own struggle against the constraints of his existence.

In this dance of power and tension, I was but a spectator, glimpsing the layers of complexity that defined the demon court.

As the tension between prince and king lingered, the atmosphere was suddenly disrupted by Behomath's voice—a calculated shift in focus that seemed intended to break the weight of the moment.

"Your Highness," Behomath's voice was smooth, the tone almost casual as he redirected the conversation towards other matters that required the king's attention. His words wove through the air like a thread of relief, dissipating the charged atmosphere that had settled over the court.

Behomath's skillful maneuver was a reminder that the demon court was a realm of shifting allegiances and intricate politics. The dynamics between prince and king were but one layer of the complexity that defined this place—a realm where power was a delicate balance, and every word spoken carried consequences that reverberated through the intricate web of power.

As the court's attention shifted towards the issues Behomath had raised, I couldn't help but feel a mixture of fascination and unease.

The truths that had begun to unravel were but glimpses into a world far more intricate and treacherous than I had ever imagined. And as I continued to navigate this realm of darkness and intrigue, I was determined to uncover the secrets that lay beneath its surface, even as the intricacies of the court continued to unfold before me.

The soft glow of candlelight flickered in my room as I sat, lost in thought. The events of the court still echoed in my mind, the complexities of the demon kingdom's dynamics a whirlwind of intrigue and tension.

A gentle knock on the door pulled me from my reverie, and as I turned towards it, Sofia's worried face appeared in the doorway. Her presence was a mixture of familiarity and comfort, a friend amidst the storm that had become my life here.

"Elvira," Sofia's voice was tinged with concern as she entered, holding something delicate and intimate in her hands. "I know you're navigating this realm with all your strength, but I... I worry for you."

Her words held a depth of sincerity that touched my heart. Sofia's friendship had been a lifeline in this unfamiliar world, and her genuine concern was a reminder that amidst the darkness, there were still bonds that held true.

"What's troubling you, Sofia?" I asked gently, my gaze meeting hers as I tried to understand the source of her anxiety.

Sofia's fingers tightened around the delicate lingerie she held, and her voice wavered slightly as she spoke. "Elvira, Kael...he's ordered that no one else is going to bed him but you."

A shiver ran down my spine at her words, a mixture of unease and uncertainty flooding my thoughts. Kael's motives had always been elusive, his actions a dance of darkness and intrigue. The notion that he was involved in my personal space brought forth a new level of complexity—one that I hadn't fully anticipated.

"He... he scares me, Elvira," Sofia's voice trembled, her worry palpable. "I've heard things about him, about his darkness. I fear what his intentions might be."

As I listened to Sofia's words, I couldn't deny the unease that settled within me. The enigma that was Kael seemed to grow deeper with each revelation. And as I grappled with the implications of his request.

"Sofia," I said softly, trying to project a reassuring tone despite my own uncertainties. "I understand your concerns, and I promise you that I will be cautious. Whatever Kael's intentions are, I will find a way to navigate them."

Sofia's eyes were wide with fear, and she clutched the lingerie tightly as if it were a lifeline. "Elvira, you don't understand. He's not like other demons. He's ruthless, and the stories... they're not just stories. Any human who has been intimate with him has... not survived. He craves pain, Elvira, not tenderness."

The weight of Sofia's words settled over us, a chilling reminder of the depths of darkness that surrounded Kael. My attempts to reassure her felt feeble in the face of such a dire reality. The enigma that was the demon prince seemed to shift and contort with every revelation, his motives a maze of complexity that left me feeling increasingly vulnerable.

"I won't let anything happen to me," I said with more determination than I felt. "I'll find a way to handle him, to protect myself."

Sofia's gaze held a mix of desperation and concern, her grip on the lingerie showing white knuckles. "Elvira, I just... I don't want you to be another victim of his darkness. Please be careful."

As I looked at my friend's worried face, I couldn't help but feel a swell of gratitude for her genuine concern. The darkness that had infiltrated the demon kingdom was a reality I couldn't ignore, and facing it head-on would require a strength and resolve that I wasn't sure I possessed. But I was determined to uncover the truths that lay hidden beneath the surface, even if it meant navigating the treacherous paths that Kael's darkness presented.

As I carefully slipped into the delicate lingerie, the fabric cool against my skin, a mix of emotions swirled within me. The mirror before me reflected an image that was both familiar and transformed—layers of uncertainty intermingled with a newfound sense of confidence.

Gazing at my own reflection, I found myself scrutinizing the contours of my features—the curve of my collarbone, the arch of my brows, the softness of my lips. In this moment, amidst the complexities of the demon court and the enigma of Kael, I allowed myself a fleeting acknowledgment of my own attractiveness.

But as I stood there, examining my reflection, a wave of apprehension washed over me. The tales of Kael's darkness, his ruthlessness, and the pain he was said to crave, lingered in my thoughts. Could the man who had shown glimpses of gentleness and complexity truly be capable of such brutality?

Hope mingled with uncertainty within me. I yearned for the Kael I had shared moments with—a Kael whose complexity hinted at something more than the darkness that surrounded him. And as I prepared myself for the night ahead, I clung to the possibility that behind closed doors, he might still be the enigmatic prince whose motives I longed to uncover.

With a steadying breath, I pushed aside the fears and doubts that threatened to consume me. The path I had chosen was one of treacherous terrain, a journey into the heart of darkness that held both danger and revelations. And as I looked at my reflection one last time, and headed to Prince Kael's chambers.

Summoning my resolve, I approached Prince Kael's chambers, my heart beating a rapid rhythm within my chest. The dimly lit hallway seemed to stretch endlessly as I walked, each step a testament to the decision I had made—an exploration of the enigma that was Kael, a journey into the unknown depths of his darkness.

My knuckles rapped against the chamber door, the sound echoing softly in the quiet corridor. The moment stretched, tension and anticipation swirling within me, until finally, the door opened. Prince Kael stood before me, his presence magnetic and unsettling as ever. His eyes met mine, holding a mixture of intrigue and challenge that sent a shiver down my spine.

"Enter," he commanded, his voice a velvety whisper that seemed to brush against my senses.

Stepping into the chamber, I couldn't help but take in the scene before me. Kael stood by the window, his form illuminated by the soft glow of moonlight filtering through the curtains. A glass of whiskey rested in his hand, its amber hue catching the light. The scent of the whiskey hung in the air, mingling with a sense of anticipation that seemed to envelop the room.

His gaze was fixed outside, as if lost in thought, and for a moment, I hesitated by the door. The air was charged with a palpable tension, an unspoken understanding that we were both on the cusp of something that defied categorization.

"Elvira," Kael's voice broke the silence, drawing my attention back to him. "Sit on the bed."

His words were a command, and I found myself walking towards the bed, each step carrying a weight of uncertainty and curiosity. As I took a seat, I couldn't shake the feeling that I was navigating a labyrinth of emotions and desires—one that promised both danger and revelation, darkness and light.

The air seemed to thicken as Kael began to move, his form illuminated by the subtle play of moonlight filtering through the room. My heart raced, anticipation and unease entwined in a complex dance within me. The weight of his presence was palpable, a force that held me captive in its magnetic pull.

With each step he took, a layer of clothing was shed, revealing the contours of his lean but built form. The fabric slid off his skin, pooling onto the floor, and in that moment, the enigma of Kael seemed to take on a new dimension. He moved with a fluid grace, a predator stalking his prey, and as his gaze remained locked onto mine, a mixture of challenge and intrigue danced in his eyes.

The distance between us closed, the tension in the room coiling tighter with every passing second. His skin was illuminated by the moonlight, the play of shadows and light revealing the sculpted planes of his body. The reality of our situation settled over me—the vulnerability of being alone with this enigmatic prince, the darkness that seemed to radiate from him, and the uncharted territory that lay ahead.

As he stood before me, with his cock erect and staring at me, his gaze piercing through the layers of my thoughts, I could feel the weight of his presence like an electric charge in the air.

My heart pounded against my chest, and a sense of vulnerability washed over me as I met Kael's intense gaze. The air seemed charged with a mixture of tension and desire, but beneath it all, a wave of trepidation surged within me. His proximity, his state of undress, and the intensity of his stare were all a potent reminder of the power dynamics at play.

Tears threatened to well up in my eyes as a whirlwind of emotions swept through me. The complexity of this moment was overwhelming—my desire to understand Kael, to navigate the darkness that surrounded him, was at odds with the unease that now gripped me. I wanted to believe that there was more to him than the stories I had heard, more to our connection than a mere transaction.

But as his eyes bore into mine, an unspoken challenge and invitation lingered in the air. A part of me wanted to give in, to succumb to the pull that seemed to exist between us. Yet, another part of me was adamant—I wanted him, yes, but not like this. I wanted our intimacy to be a choice driven by mutual affection, a connection that transcended the boundaries of his darkness.

The conflict within me raged—a battle between desire and self-preservation. The fear of being used, of losing my agency, weighed heavily on my mind.

Kael brings his thumb over my lips and roughly traces them. As Kael's touch grazed my lips, a mixture of sensations cascaded through me. His fingers traced a path that was both intimate and unsettling, a reminder of the complex dance of emotions that bound us in this moment. And then, his lips met mine in a kiss that was both forceful and consuming.

My heart raced, caught between the desire that had simmered within me and the overwhelming flood of emotions that now threatened to consume me.

But as the kiss deepened, as his intensity enveloped me, I found myself losing control. The weight of everything—the darkness of his realm, the complexities of our connection, the stories I had heard—crashed down on me, and the dam holding back my emotions burst. Tears streamed down my cheeks, mingling with the sensation of his lips on mine.

And then, as if attuned to the shift in my emotions, Kael pulled away, his grip firm on my jaw. His gaze held mine, his dark eyes searching, as if seeking to unravel the turmoil that now lay bare before him. It was a vulnerable moment, a collision of raw emotions that stripped away the facade I had tried to maintain.

"Stop crying. It's displeasing."

The words hung in the air, a reminder that even in this vulnerable exchange, the dynamics of power and control remained. The rawness of my emotions, the tears that had spilled forth, were met with a jarring demand to suppress them—an expectation that the complexities of my feelings could be neatly pushed aside at his behest.

"What are you thinking so much about?"

I felt a pang of unease. How could I articulate the maelstrom of thoughts that had been triggered by this encounter? The layers of my emotions—the desire, the fear, the curiosity, and the need to understand—seemed too intricate to be reduced to words.

The tears continued to stream down my cheeks, a visual testament to the emotions that I could no longer suppress. I searched his eyes, my own filled with a mixture of uncertainty and yearning.

The darkness that surrounded him was complex, his actions and reputation at odds with the vulnerability that seemed to flicker beneath the surface.

"I don't know what to think," I admitted softly, my voice catching as the weight of the truth settled over me. "You're an enigma, Kael. Stories and shadows paint a picture, but I've seen glimpses of something more within you. And yet, I'm lost in the maze of your complexity."

In one fluid motion, Kael's demeanor shifted from an enigmatic conversation to an assertive action. His hand found its way to my waist, and before I could react, he lifted me effortlessly, his strength evident in the way he handled me. My body collided with the softness of the bed, the impact sending a jolt through me.

I looked up at him, my heart racing from both surprise and a rush of adrenaline. The intensity in his eyes hadn't wavered—it was as if his actions were an extension of the raw power he exuded. His gaze bore into mine, a mix of challenge and curiosity that seemed to defy the boundary between control and submission.

"What are you doing, Kael?" My voice quivered, a blend of apprehension and intrigue. The sudden change in dynamics had left me off balance, unsure of his intentions or the direction this encounter was taking.

He didn't respond with words. Instead, his fingers deftly traced a path along my jawline, his touch igniting a cascade of sensations that sent shivers down my spine. His gaze held mine, unwavering and intense, as if he was exploring the depths of my thoughts, my desires, and the unspoken tension that hung between us.

The seconds stretched, the air charged with anticipation. And then, without breaking eye contact, he leaned down, his lips dangerously close to mine. The space between us was electric, a magnetism that defied the conventional rules of engagement.

As our breaths mingled, his voice was a soft rumble, a testament to the complexity of our connection. "You think too much, Elvira." The words were a murmur against my lips, his breath warm and inviting.

In the fraction of a moment, the intensity of our exchange seemed to shift once again. Kael's lips, which had been dangerously close to mine, retreated, leaving an echo of his words hanging in the air. The warmth of his breath, the murmur of his voice, seemed to linger against my skin even as he held me close.

And then, as if the tide had turned, his arms enveloped me in a tight embrace. The sensation of his body pressed against mine was a stark contrast to the charged atmosphere that had defined our interactions. His hold was possessive yet oddly comforting, a juxtaposition that left me momentarily stunned.

As the weight of his presence pressed against me, a myriad of emotions surged through me. Confusion battled with curiosity, desire with uncertainty. The lines between us had been fluid from the moment we crossed paths, and now, as he held me close in an embrace that defied definition, the complexity of our connection seemed to deepen.

I lay there, my heart still racing, grappling with the enigma that was Kael. The vulnerability he had shown, the darkness he exuded, the moments of tenderness juxtaposed against cruelty—it was a puzzle that defied simple interpretation.

"You're not going to fuck me? Isn't it what you wanted? For the deal I had made with you?" I asked with a caution note.

Kael's chuckle vibrated against my ear, his breath warm against my skin as he nuzzled into the crook of my neck. "Do you want me to?" He asked.

"No." I said, I could feel my body going stiff while I answered his question.

"You think I'm that predictable?" His voice was a low murmur, his lips brushing against my skin in a way that sent a shiver down my spine. His proximity was intoxicating, a reminder of the fine line we walked between desire and uncertainty.

My breath caught at his question, my words hanging in the air for a moment. "I don't know what to expect from you, Kael. This realm, these dynamics—they're beyond anything I've known."

His response was a husky chuckle, his fingers tracing patterns against my skin with a touch that was both tender and tantalizing. "And yet, here you are, nestled against me. Do you regret it?"

The question lingered, hanging in the air like a challenge. I hesitated, my thoughts a whirlwind of conflicting emotions. "Regret? No," I admitted, my voice a mixture of honesty and uncertainty. "But that doesn't mean I understand everything, Kael."

He placing his lips on my shoulder, laying gentle kisses.

"You didn't answer my question, why didn't you fuck me? when you could and no one would stop you." I asked stopping my tears that again threatened to flow.

"You're different," his voice a whisper against my skin. "You challenge the norm, the expectations. You're not just another plaything."

I shifted in his embrace, my thoughts churning as I tried to make sense of the complexity of our interactions. His admission was a reminder that beneath the enigma and darkness, there was a person with his own set of desires and conflicts—a person who defied categorization.

But then, as if to contrast the tenderness of his words, he added with a teasing edge, "And crying out of pain doesn't suit you, Elvira. I prefer to cry out of pleasure beneath me. Withering in my hold, eager to please me."

Epilogue

As the morning light filtered through the curtains, casting a gentle glow across the room, I found myself entwined with Kael in a way that felt both surreal and intimate. The memories of the night's conversations and emotions lingered in the air like a whispered promise—a promise of complexity and understanding that seemed to defy the boundaries of this realm.

My fingers traced the mark he had left on me days ago, the teeth prints etched onto my skin. It was a reminder of the depths to which our interactions had taken us, a testament to the intertwining of darkness and connection that defined our journey. The faint silver line that bordered the mark seemed to hold a quiet significance, a symbol of the intricacies that lay beneath the surface.

As I shifted to face him, his features softened in the morning light, the lines of his face accentuated by shadows and highlights. I watched him sleep, his chest rising and falling with a steady rhythm, a reminder of the vulnerability that sleep often unveiled in even the most enigmatic of beings.

My thoughts danced between the moments we had shared—the darkness, the vulnerability, the unexpected tenderness. It was a tapestry woven with threads of desire and complexity, a tapestry that both intrigued and challenged me.

I knew that our connection wasn't straightforward, that the road ahead was shrouded in uncertainties. But as I looked at Kael's slumbering form, I couldn't deny the pull of my own emotions. There was a part of me that craved to unravel the layers that surrounded him, to understand the enigma beneath the surface.

With a sigh, I settled back against the pillows, my gaze lingering on his sleeping form. As I traced the curve of Kael's jawline with the gentlest touch, I couldn't help but admire the contours of his face. The sharp angles, the play of light and shadow, all seemed to come together in a portrait of contrasts—much like the enigmatic prince himself.

His features, usually marred by a veneer of darkness and intrigue, appeared softer in the morning light. The tension that often defined his demeanor seemed to ease in slumber, leaving behind a vulnerability that few were privy to witness. It was as if sleep revealed a side of him that was hidden from the world—an unguarded glimpse into the complexities that lay beneath the surface.

As my fingertip traced the line of his jaw, I found myself captivated by the dichotomy that defined him. The darkness and the tenderness, the desire and the vulnerability—it was a tapestry that I was just beginning to understand. And in this quiet moment, as I gazed upon his sleeping form, I couldn't deny the growing connection between us—a connection that defied categorization and challenged the very fabric of our worlds.

The morning sunlight painted his features with a warm hue, casting a gentle radiance that seemed to highlight the nuances of his expression. And as my touch lingered on his skin, I was startled by the subtle movement beneath my fingertips. Kael's lips curved into a small, almost imperceptible smile, as if he was attuned to the sensation even in his slumber. The sight of his smile, a rare vulnerability that played across his features, sent a rush of warmth through me.

Embarrassment tinged my cheeks as I realized that he was aware, even in sleep, of my presence and my touch. It was a reminder that the boundaries between us were fluid, that even in the quiet intimacy of this moment, a connection existed that defied explanation.

And then, as if prompted by his own subconscious desire, Kael shifted slightly, nudging me with a gentle movement. The contact between us grew, and I felt the weight of his body press against mine—a touch that was both tender and electrifying. The warmth of his proximity, the way his body responded to my touch, sent a rush of tingling sensations through me.

It was as if he was urging me to explore, to trace the contours of his skin with the same curiosity that had led me to this point.

With a mixture of reluctance and longing, I finally withdrew my touch from his skin, a soft sigh escaping my lips. I shifted slightly on the bed, my gaze drifting to the sunlight streaming through the window. "I should get ready for work," I whispered, my voice carrying a note of regret.

Kael's response was a low, amused rumble. "Work, in my chambers? That's a new excuse, Elvira."

A playful smile tugged at the corners of my lips as I met his gaze, finding myself caught in the magnetic pull of his eyes. "You know what I mean. I have responsibilities outside of this room."

His laughter was a rich melody that filled the space between us, a sound that was equal parts teasing and intoxicating. "Of course, my dear Elvira. Don't let me keep you from your important work."

I rolled my eyes, a mixture of exasperation and affection warming my expression. "Believe it or not, there's more to my life than this."

He grinned, the playful spark in his eyes igniting a flutter in my chest. "I find that hard to believe, considering how captivated you seem by my charming presence."

I couldn't help but chuckle, the tension that had simmered between us slowly dissipating. "You're impossible."

He stretched leisurely on the bed, a cat-like grace in his movements. "And you're intriguing, Elvira. But go on, tend to your responsibilities. I'll be here when you return. Oh and I enjoy waking up like this...having you naked and pressed against my body."

Turning back to face him, I met his gaze with a mixture of bashfulness and something else—something that I couldn't quite put into words. "You enjoy waking up with me... like this?"

His grin was a mixture of mischief and genuine appreciation. "Naked against my body? Yes, Elvira, I find it rather... enjoyable."

The candidness of his response made me both self-conscious and surprisingly pleased. The idea that he found comfort in our closeness, that he derived a sense of satisfaction from the moments we shared, was a revelation that sent a warm flutter through my chest.

"Is that so?" I replied, my voice carrying a note of playful skepticism.

He lifted himself onto his elbows, his gaze never leaving mine. "You're exquisite, Elvira. A sight that's more captivating than any morning sun."

The sincerity of his words took me by surprise, the intensity of his gaze holding a depth of emotion that both thrilled and unsettled me. In the span of a few heartbeats, I felt a whirlwind of emotions—gratitude, vulnerability, and an undeniable pull towards this enigmatic being who had come to occupy a significant space in my life.

I shook my head, a mixture of disbelief and a hint of embarrassment coloring my expression. "You have a way with words, Kael." I retorted wearing my robe.

He chuckled softly, his gaze softening as he held my gaze. "Only when they're true, Elvira."

The weight of his gaze, the honesty in his words, held a gravity that was impossible to ignore. In that moment, I couldn't help but feel that our connection was a complex dance—a dance of contrasts and contradictions, of darkness and light, of vulnerability and strength.

As I entered my room, a wave of relief washed over me, and I could feel the tension slowly easing from my shoulders. But my moment of solitude was short-lived, as I saw Sofia anxiously sitting on my bed. Her eyes were wide with worry, and before I could say a word, she flung herself onto me in a tight embrace.

"Elvira! Oh, thank the heavens you're safe," Sofia's voice trembled as she held me, her grip almost desperate in its intensity.

I returned the embrace, my heart warming at her genuine concern. "Sofia, I'm here. I'm fine."

Sofia pulled back slightly, her hands still holding onto me as if afraid to let go. Her eyes were filled with unshed tears, and I could see the depth of her anxiety etched across her features.

"You went... You went and spent the night at Prince Kael's chambers," Sofia's voice quivered as she spoke. "I was so scared for you, Elvira. He's known for his darkness, for his cruelty..."

I gently cupped her face, my fingers brushing away a tear that had escaped her eye. "Sofia, I promise you, I'm alright. Nothing happened to me."

Her gaze searched mine, as if seeking the truth in my words. "But he's different, Elvira. He's not like the others. I've heard things, things that make my blood run cold. He had taken an entire army all by himself. There was this she-demon who wanted to bed him during the blood moon time and when she did, everyone could hear her screams in the palace and those screams weren't of pleasure."

I sighed softly, understanding her concern. Kael's reputation within the demon kingdom was complex, a mixture of fear and intrigue that had only deepened since I'd become entangled with him.

"Sofia, I know he's... enigmatic, to say the least," I began, choosing my words carefully. "But there's more to him than meets the eye. I've seen different sides of him, and I believe there's a reason for his actions."

Sofia's grip on me loosened slightly, and she looked at me with a mixture of uncertainty and hope. "You... you really believe that?"

I nodded, a small smile tugging at my lips. "I do. And I promise you, I'll be cautious. But I also want to understand him better, to uncover the truth behind his actions."

Sofia took a deep breath, her anxiety slowly giving way to a glimmer of relief. "Just... promise me you'll be careful, Elvira. I don't want to lose you."

Touched by her concern, I hugged her tightly once more. "I promise, Sofia. I'll be careful. And I'll always come back to you."

As we held onto each other, I couldn't help but feel grateful for Sofia's friendship—the unwavering support and genuine care she offered. In a realm of darkness and uncertainty, her presence was a guiding light that reminded me of the importance of human connection and empathy.